D0175706

"You're not a bad ho

Jeremy chuckled and stood up, pushing his chair back under the table. "You mean you don't mind that I've invaded your family dinners and movie nights?" Jeremy's smile caused tingles to crawl up her neck.

"Not to mention the fact that you've fixed things around the house," Alison began, "taught my son to fly-fish, been gracious enough to stay longer in order to enter a chili cook-off, and I just caught you washing dishes—I don't mind, Jeremy."

His chuckle faded and he moved to stand right in front of her. "Having you here has been…" Alison froze and couldn't finish her thought.

"I keep telling myself not to like you so much," he said quietly. "It's not working."

A roller coaster of emotions plummeted inside of Alison.

"I feel the same way," she admitted. She tried to concentrate on breathing but Jeremy's close proximity seemed to make that impossible.

"Can I kiss you, Alison?" he asked, his voice just above a whisper as he leaned down toward her. Alison closed her eyes.

"Yes," she whispered.

Books by Brandy Bruce

Love Inspired Heartsong Presents

Table for Two
Second Chance Café
Recipe for Love

BRANDY BRUCE

is a wife, mother, editor, author and someone who really loves dessert. She started scribbling stories in spiral notebooks when she was twelve years old, and her love for books never left her. Brandy makes her home in Colorado with her husband, Jeff, her daughter, Ashtyn, and her son, Lincoln. When she's not editing manuscripts or writing stories, she loves reading, watching movies based on Jane Austen novels, spending time with her family and baking any kind of cheesecake. She loves hearing from readers. You can contact her through her blog at www.brandybruce.blogspot.com.

BRANDY BRUCE

Recipe for Love

HEARTSONG
PRESENTS

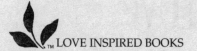

LOVE INSPIRED BOOKS

PLEASE RECYCLE
THIS PRODUCT IS RECYCLABLE

Recycling programs
for this product may
not exist in your area.

ISBN-13: 978-0-373-48735-6

Recipe for Love

www.Harlequin.com

Printed in U.S.A.

Behold, God is my salvation. I will trust, and will not be afraid; for the Lord God is my strength and my song, and he has become my salvation.
—*Isaiah* 12:2

For Jeff, Ashtyn and Lincoln—
I love you with all my heart.

Acknowledgments

Kathy Davis, my editor and friend.
This is the second time in my life that you've been
instrumental in making one of my dreams come true.
I am so very blessed to know you and am grateful
for your friendship.

Chip MacGregor, when we first met you told me you
took on people, not projects. That was one hundred
percent true. Thank you for your belief in me.

Thank you so much to my parents and my sisters,
who always love and support me. I couldn't finish
anything without you. I am blessed beyond measure
to have such a wonderful family. To my husband, Jeff,
your confidence in me gives me the ability to
keep dreaming. Thank you. Ashtyn and Lincoln,
thank you for smiles and hugs and kisses and love
and for being mine.

Many thanks to my sweet grandmother Mimi.
You hold a special place in my heart,
and I carry your love and faith in me wherever I go.

Chapter 1

Jeremy Mitchell gritted his teeth as his cell phone lost service again, along with his GPS navigation. He slowed to see the name of the next road.

"It would have been nice to know that there isn't reliable cell service this far up into the mountains," he muttered.

The road narrowed, and despite his frustration that his GPS wasn't working, Jeremy drank in the scenery. He'd left Denver hours ago for Estes Park, Colorado, for this very reason—beauty and peace. He wanted to experience the sunshine of the days and sharp chill of the nights as the mountains transitioned into autumn. The aspen trees, many of which had already changed to yellow hues, the magnificent colors of the flowers, the clear mountain air, the cold rushing water of the rivers and waterfalls—he wanted all of it.

Jeremy breathed a sigh of relief when he saw the turn for Rockridge Lane. After driving about a mile down the gravel road, he saw a large, worn sign that read Mountain View Bed & Breakfast. He pulled into the circular drive, came to a stop and took a moment to look at the two-story house in front of him. It needed a fresh coat of paint; that was for sure. But the B&B sat right by a river, and that was all Jeremy needed. Well, that and a fly-fishing rod. With it being late September, quality fishing opportunities would be winding down as winter approached. He hopped out of his truck, grabbed his luggage and gear and headed up the front porch steps.

He knocked three times and waited. The door opened and a boy who could be no older than seven or eight stood in front of him. They just stared at each other.

"Is your mom home?" Jeremy asked.

"Nicholas!" A slim, blond-haired woman came rushing up behind the boy. "You know you're not supposed to open the door without me! Oh! Hi there. I'm Alison Taylor. You must be Jeremy Mitchell. Please come in. This is my son, Nicholas." She opened the door wider as she gestured toward her son.

Nicholas held out his hand. "I just turned eight."

Jeremy bit back a chuckle and gave the boy's hand a good shake. "Nice to meet you, Nicholas."

He stepped inside the foyer and took a look around. It looked like most B&Bs Jeremy had stayed at in the past—a little quaint, a little rustic and old-fashioned, but neat, clean and welcoming. He set down his bags and pulled out the online registration form he'd printed. Alison took it from him.

"Thanks so much. Well, let me show you to your room."

Nicholas reached for one of the smaller bags. "I'll help you, Mister."

"Thanks. You can call me Jeremy, if that's okay with your mom."

"It's fine," Alison said amiably. She headed up the staircase, and Jeremy and Nicholas followed her. "You're our only guest this week, Jeremy, so please make yourself at home. Breakfast is at eight, unless you'd prefer to have it earlier. You mentioned in your email that you plan on doing a lot of fishing. I can work with your schedule." Alison took a right at the top of the stairs and stopped.

"Three rooms are up here—the Dove, the Ark and the Haven. I prepared the Dove for you because it has the best view, but the Ark is bigger and you can certainly have that room if you'd like the extra space. The Haven is the smallest room of the three. All three rooms have telephones that ring downstairs to our living quarters, so you can call anytime you need to. And each bedroom has its own private bath."

"The Dove sounds fine, Mrs. Taylor. Thank you," Jeremy said. She nodded and opened the door to her right. Nicholas walked in first and set down the bag he was carrying.

"Please call me Alison. And…" Alison hesitated for a moment, her eyes on Nicholas. "You might as well know that I'm a widow."

Jeremy's mouth went dry. "I'm so sorry."

"Thank you." She held out a single key. "Here's a key to the front door. I keep it locked most of the time, so please always keep the key on you. You are welcome to the snacks on the kitchen counter. Please make yourself at home." She smiled. "Our primary living space is in the basement, so the first-floor living room and dining areas are available for your use. Also, the river is very close. You can see it from our breakfast area downstairs. You can go right out the back door, off the deck and make your way to the water. I assume you have a fishing license?"

"Of course," Jeremy responded as he set his rod in the corner of the room. Nicholas stood next to his mother and she ruffled his hair affectionately.

"All right then, Jeremy. Welcome to the Mountain View B&B," Alison said.

"We hope your stay is a nice one," Nicholas chimed in. Alison beamed at him, and then the two of them descended the stairs, leaving Jeremy to get settled.

"I don't want to have to tell you again, Nic. You have to wait for me before you open the door to strangers. Got it?" Alison stood at the bottom of the stairs with her hands on her hips. Her son hung his head and looked appropriately reprimanded.

"Sorry, Mom. I've got it."

Alison leaned down so that the two of them were eye level. "It's my job to protect you. It's just you and me here, and I need you to listen to me. The people who stay with us are our guests, but we don't really know them. We need to be cautious. That means you follow the rules I set."

"Okay. Jeremy seems nice, though, doesn't he?"

Alison straightened and gave her son a smile. "Sure he does. I hope he has a good time here." At the sound of a car turning into the driveway, Alison peered through the front window. "Grandpa's here. Go grab your hoodie. Remember, he's taking you to Griffin's birthday party and then bringing you home. I'd like you to be home in time for dinner."

Nicholas was already running toward the basement stairs to grab his sweatshirt. Alison opened the front door and stood on the porch as her dad jumped out of his Yukon.

"Hi, Dad," she called out, preparing herself for the questions that he would undoubtedly ask about the truck parked in front of the house.

"Do you have a guest?" he asked. She glued a smile on her face.

"We sure do. Isn't that great?"

He frowned. "Did a couple come up to the mountains for the weekend or is it a family with kids?"

She shook her head. "No. Actually, it's just a fisherman. He'll be staying with us for the week."

Her dad's frown deepened. She didn't blame him. In all honesty, having a stranger stay with her and Nicholas for the week wasn't an ideal situation and she knew it. But with their current financial state, Alison couldn't be choosy about guests. She kept the door to the basement locked and Connor's old handgun in her closet, and she tried to vet her guests as much as possible before agreeing to let them stay. She never allowed Nicholas to be alone with the guests unless they were children his age or younger.

She ran a B&B, after all. She had to entertain guests or she might as well close up and sell now. Her parents had recommended she do just that after Connor died, but Alison hadn't been able to bring herself to sell the business that she and Connor had started together.

She'd lost Connor, her best friend and the love of her life. She couldn't bear to lose the dream they'd shared of owning their own business. Not to mention the fact that they'd invested every penny they owned in the B&B. Alison avoided eye contact with her dad, hoping to steer clear of any disapproval he might show for her decisions.

"Thanks for taking Nicholas to the birthday party, Dad. I appreciate it. Here are the directions to get to Griffin's house." She walked down the porch steps and handed him a map she'd printed off the Internet.

"I don't mind at all," her father said and Alison believed him. Her parents lived in a small house right outside of town, and they spent as much time with Nicholas as possible. Alison's dad especially tried to make time for him since Connor had passed away, and that meant the world to Alison.

Nicholas came running out the door and down the steps. "Hi, Grandpa!"

Her father's eyes lit up. "Hey, champ!"

"Did you get the gift for Griffin?" Alison asked, and Nicholas held up the gift bag with the baseball cap Nicholas had chosen for his friend.

"All right then. Have fun! I'll see you at dinnertime."

Alison waved from the porch as they drove off and then just stood for a moment, enjoying the sound of the wind whistling through the trees. When the door behind her opened, she jumped.

"Did I scare you?" Jeremy asked. Alison tried to catch her breath.

"No. Well, maybe a little. I'm not that used to having people around." Alison wanted to bite her tongue. *I run a bed and breakfast, for crying out loud!* She scolded herself.

Jeremy's face didn't show any emotion. "Things have been slow?" he asked.

You could say that, Alison thought dryly. *You're my first guest in more than a month.*

"Yes, but I'm hoping things will pick up. A lot of people like to visit the mountains when the colors change."

He nodded. "I had hoped you could recommend a few restaurants in the area."

They stood rather awkwardly on the porch with Jeremy framed in the doorway and Alison by the steps.

"Absolutely. If you want to go back inside, I have some Estes Park brochures with lists of restaurants, local attractions—basically anything and everything about the surrounding area."

Jeremy stepped aside, letting her go through the front door first. Alison tried to ignore the unease she felt. It had been a long time since she'd been alone with a man—other than her dad, of course.

"Here they are," she said once they reached the kitchen. She showed him the basket where she kept brochures for the guests.

"And what do *you* recommend?" Jeremy asked pointedly. Alison thought for a moment. She and Nicholas rarely went out to eat. But she'd lived in Estes Park since high school, so she knew the area well.

"For such a small town, we have lots of restaurants to choose from. Do you like Italian food?"

Alison caught the amused look on Jeremy's face when she said that, but he didn't elaborate so she didn't ask.

"I do," he answered.

"Mama Rose's is good. Dave's BBQ is another local favorite."

"Is it okay for me to use the kitchen on evenings I'm here?" Jeremy asked.

"Of course. Nicholas and I usually have our meals downstairs when guests are here. I have a kitchenette in the basement. But even if I do cook upstairs, Nic and I will eat downstairs. For the most part, the kitchen is available to you. I'm afraid none of the local places deliver way out here. We're just a little far for that."

"No problem."

They stood in silence for a moment, then Jeremy pulled out one of the bar stools and sat down at the peninsula counter, flipping through the pamphlets.

"I was about to make some coffee. Would you like some?" Alison offered. He looked up.

"That sounds great. I was thinking I'd take a walk down to the river in a bit. Sort of scout out my trail for tomorrow."

Good coffee was the one pricy treat Alison splurged on. The B&B had had a few busy weeks midsummer, but spring had been too slow. Too many weeks without any income. Connor's life insurance had kept her afloat so far, but she'd set aside money for Nicholas's college fund and refused to touch that. The funds she had reserved to supplement her income were dwindling quickly. She had no money for extras. But on the bad days, on the days when she missed Connor the most, a good cup of coffee comforted her.

Within minutes, the smell of fresh coffee filled the kitchen. "Good coffee," Jeremy murmured once Alison had poured and handed him a mug. He breathed in the scent approvingly. "You have a lovely home," he said as he walked over by the windows and looked out.

The breakfast area and the connecting living room were surrounded by large windows, which was just one of the reasons Alison and Connor had fallen in love with the B&B the first time they'd walked through it. The windows let in the life of the mountains. Through the trees, one could see the river rushing. Deer and elk would often meander within arm's length of the house.

"Thank you. I have ideas for improvements…but well, like I mentioned before, things have been slow." Alison knew the house badly needed to be repainted. And the interior was dated and needed redecorating. But she was too strapped financially to spend much money on the house.

"Everything looks nice. And the location is really the best feature. I'd love to buy a place like this someday—tucked away in the mountains, next to a river," Jeremy stated.

"I love it here," Alison said. "My family moved to Estes Park from Denver when I was sixteen. I thought I'd hate it, but I couldn't have been more wrong. I fell in love with the area. I can't imagine ever leaving."

Alison wanted to clamp her mouth shut. *Why do I keep rambling? Am I so desperate for conversation? Why not just wear a sign that reads, "I'm lonely!" Stop telling him such personal things.*

But Jeremy didn't seem annoyed. "I moved to Denver from Santa Fe to go to college, and I ended up staying," he told her. "I enjoy the city, but I come up to the mountains whenever I can. It's peaceful. Something about being on the river makes me feel closer to God."

Alison understood the feeling. "I found my soul when my family settled here. I'd go hiking with my dad and come across a waterfall or a river, and it's like I could feel God speaking peace over me. I'd never felt so close to Him before. Am I right in assuming you're a believer, too, then?" Alison ventured, hoping she wasn't overstepping by asking.

"Yes. I've been a believer since grade school. But life can get so hectic—sometimes I have to take myself out of my schedule in order to reconnect with God."

"So…your soul is thirsting for a river?" she said knowingly, and Jeremy smiled.

"I couldn't have said it more perfectly."

He looked back toward the view, and Alison took that moment to *really* look over Jeremy Mitchell. He probably wasn't much older than her—maybe in his early to mid thirties. His light blond hair was cropped short and his hazel eyes were friendly, though a little serious. He stood with perfect posture; Alison wondered if he came from a military household. He was dressed for the mountains with brown boots, a red flannel shirt and dark jeans.

He seemed to be about Connor's height and build, maybe six foot or six foot one and fit. He looked like someone who lifted weights on a regular basis. But that's where the similarities with Connor ended. Connor's Hispanic heritage gave him olive skin, dark hair and even darker eyes. And Connor's eyes were almost always playful. He was a jokester, rarely serious.

But in that moment, watching Jeremy Mitchell, Alison didn't mind the seriousness that seemed to accompany him. He was handsome in an earthy way that Alison liked. He turned back toward her.

"Thank you for the coffee, Alison."

She froze at the sound of her name on his lips.

Oh, dear.

Jeremy left the mug in the sink and then took off out the back door to explore. Alison stood unmoving in the kitchen, rationalizing away her attraction to this hazel-eyed stranger.

It's been two years since Connor died—obviously I'm lonely. I've been so preoccupied with taking care of Nicholas and running the business that I haven't had much of a social life. I'm stressed about money and I miss the life I had with Connor. So I'm reacting to even the smallest attention from an attractive man. It's nothing.

From where she stood, she could see Jeremy navigate the rocky riverbank as he followed the river west.

Oh Lord, help me to get a grip.

Chapter 2

As the sky darkened over the mountains, leaving the glow of the most breathtaking sunset Jeremy had seen in months, he leaned against a tree and listened to the soothing sounds of the river. A rumble in his stomach reminded him that dinnertime was near. But he'd been waiting for this moment for too long to let it go just yet.

He closed his eyes.

God, I need solace. I need You to meet me here.

Life as the executive chef at Romano's in downtown Denver didn't leave much room for stillness. At this moment, feeling the chill of evening and hearing the water flow, Jeremy didn't miss the hustle and bustle of the restaurant kitchen at all. He'd miss it eventually, no doubt, but right now he needed to nourish that place inside his soul that longed for peace and quiet.

Jeremy pushed himself away from the tree, went to the riverbank and reached down to let the frigid water rush over his fingers. He then walked parallel to the river, taking note of what insects were hatching on the water and considering which flies he would use for fishing the next morning. He studied the river, checking for both deep pockets and places where the waterway rippled. Standing beneath a fall covering of trees, sensing the river's pulse as it ebbed and flowed, Jeremy itched to grab his rod and flies and cast a line.

I think I've needed this for longer than I realized.

Other than quick trips down to Santa Fe to see his mom and sister, Jeremy hadn't taken a real vacation in years. He'd worked as a short-order cook, then as a sous chef for several years and finally, as an executive chef. When Leonardo Romano had hired him to be the head chef at one of his two Romano's locations, Jeremy had known that he'd just gotten any chef's dream job. To work at the well-respected and popular Romano's, cooking authentic Italian cuisine, was the opportunity of a lifetime, at least for Jeremy. It was what he'd worked toward during those years studying in culinary school and cooking in smaller restaurants, trying to build up his reputation. And he loved it. He loved the fast pace and the challenge.

But a few weeks ago he'd hit the pinnacle of exhaustion. It was on August 27th, the fifth anniversary of his father's death. How could it already have been five years since his father had lost his battle with prostate cancer? Jeremy had grieved when his father passed away, of course, but he had tried to stay strong for his mom and his younger sister, June. But this year the anniversary hit him differently. He thought of the fishing trips he'd taken with his father. His dad had loved to fish.

Jeremy had felt it deep inside him, an almost desperate need to be near a river. So he'd booked a room at a river-side B&B for a week and left the city behind him. Now here he was, taking a much-needed vacation.

Jeremy dusted off his jeans and headed back to the B&B, his thoughts drifting to his hostess, Alison Taylor, and her son, Nicholas. Maybe only because he understood all too well, he'd recognized the weariness in Alison. He'd heard the tremble in her voice when she talked about the B&B having had few guests. The anxiety and weight on her shoulders came through as clear as day to Jeremy.

He couldn't help wondering what had happened to her husband. But he hadn't wanted to pry. Still, he hoped she might tell him eventually.

As he approached the house, he noticed that the kitchen and eating area were lit up. He stopped for a minute, taking in the sight of Alison and Nicholas. She stood at the stove while Nicholas sat perched on a barstool. Even from a distance Jeremy could see the animation in Nicholas's face as he talked to his mom. Jeremy couldn't hear it, but he could tell she was laughing out loud.

Jeremy grinned as he watched Alison laugh. He hadn't realized how pretty she was. She looked out at that moment, and the smile froze on her face. Nicholas turned to follow her gaze and waved to Jeremy. Jeremy waved back and quickened his step to the back deck, feeling more than a little embarrassed that he'd been caught watching them.

Nicholas met him at the door. "Hi, Jeremy!"

Jeremy grinned at the boy. "Hi again." He glanced up at Alison. "Something smells good in here."

Alison wiped her hands on a dishtowel. "I was just throwing together something for dinner. We'll be heading downstairs soon."

Jeremy shook his head. "There's no need for that. I'm going to drive into town, so please, feel free to just stay up here and eat."

"We're having spaghetti. Mom, is there enough for Jeremy?" If she hadn't been obviously mortified, Jeremy would have thought the deep-red flush on her cheeks was attractive.

"Um, well..." Alison stuttered.

Jeremy shook his head. "That's okay, buddy. I need to run into town anyway."

Nicholas's face fell and Jeremy felt awful. He stole a look at Alison and realized she was watching the same thing. He could almost see her mentally considering her options.

"It's up to you, of course, Jeremy, but there's plenty. I can make you a plate, if you want."

"Yeah! Stay and eat with us!" Nicholas exclaimed.

Jeremy couldn't exactly say no at that point.

"What can I do to help?" he asked.

"You guys set the table," Alison instructed. Within fifteen minutes, the three of them were sitting together at the table. Alison prayed over the food, a simple prayer thanking God for bringing Jeremy to their house, but it touched Jeremy. Then Nicholas rambled on about the birthday party he'd attended that afternoon.

"We had pizza for lunch. Pizza was dad's favorite, right, Mom?" Nicholas suddenly said.

Alison paled. "That's right, Nic. He loved pizza."

Nicholas kept right on talking, but Jeremy felt Alison's mood shift.

How on earth did I get into this position? I came here to be alone. It's my first night and I'm already participating in family dinner, eating spaghetti and listening to the rundown of a child's birthday party.

With barely a breath between switching gears, Nicholas asked Jeremy what kind of fishing he planned to do, which segued into myriad questions regarding fly-fishing and a story about Nicholas having once seen a trout jump *at least* six inches before falling back in the river.

"So, what do you do, Jeremy?" Alison asked after sternly telling Nicholas to eat and to please stop talking so much.

"I'm a chef."

Alison's eyes widened in surprise. "You're telling me that tomorrow morning I'll be cooking breakfast for a chef? That a chef is eating my overcooked spaghetti and Ragú?"

Jeremy laughed out loud. "No pressure. I'll be thankful for whatever you make. And I thought the spaghetti was great."

Alison blushed, and just like when he saw her laugh, Jeremy was struck by how attractive she was. Her light blond hair fell in soft wisps around her face and cascaded down well below her shoulders. Her brown eyes seemed to convey anxiety, exhaustion, concern and hope all in one look that Jeremy found particularly intriguing.

"Where do you cook?" Alison wondered.

"A family-owned restaurant in Denver called Romano's. There are two of them actually. Well, three, I guess, if you count the one in Los Angeles. But my boss only owns the two Denver locations. I cook for the 15th Street location. I've been there for more than four years now."

"Are you married?" Nicholas asked, and Alison's face burned red again.

"Nicholas! Please stop talking," she said in a high, frustrated tone.

Jeremy tried to cover his laughter by coughing. "Um, no. I'm not married. I'm too busy working to have a wife."

Nicholas seemed to think this over. "You're not working right now."

Good point. And this is getting a little awkward.

Alison cleared her throat. "Nic, that's enough. It's your night to do the dishes. Maybe you should get started."

Nicholas groaned and dragged himself from the table, taking as long as possible to reach the kitchen sink. Jeremy and Alison both cleared the table and Jeremy offered to help with the dishes, but Alison wasn't having it.

"You're probably thinking you picked the wrong B&B for your relaxing week in the mountains," Alison said.

Jeremy shook his head. "Not at all. I appreciate you two including me tonight. Not to mention feeding me!"

Alison gave him a small smile. "It was nice to have you join us."

After bedtime prayers, Alison took the opportunity to insist that Nicholas not ask such personal questions of their guest. She perched on the edge of Nicholas's bed as he kicked the covers off and flattened his pillow—Nicholas's nightly routine. Alison would've smiled at the predictable habit if she hadn't felt so determined to address boundaries.

"He's here to fish, Nic. And to take a break from his job. We need to give him the space he came here for."

She didn't miss the disappointment on Nicholas's face, but Alison stayed firm.

"It's nice having Jeremy around. Like at dinner. It was like having a dad," Nicholas said wistfully. Alison felt like she'd been sucker-punched.

Should've seen that coming, but I didn't. Oh, Nic! I'm so sorry, kiddo.

Alison brushed Nicholas's dark hair from his forehead, looking for traces of Connor in his face. For a silent moment, her heart searched for the right words to say to her son.

"Nicholas, I miss your dad too. But Jeremy's just a visitor. He's paying to stay here, and we need to be good hosts. Be polite, and you can talk to him if he has time, but remember that we don't really know him. He's just a nice man who's staying for a few days."

"Yes, Mom." Nicholas sighed.

After closing the door to Nicholas's room and making herself a cup of tea, Alison curled up on the small sofa in the basement and flipped through the TV channels, trying to distract herself from replaying the evening's events in her mind. She thought about Jeremy's pleasant demeanor even when faced with a rather awkward situation. Alison just shook her head, frustrated by how the evening had played out. At the same time, she'd be lying if she didn't admit that having someone join them for dinner was nice.

We probably didn't come across as very professional tonight. Jeremy Mitchell's most likely upstairs right now wishing he'd picked a different B&B.

Then again, maybe not. He hadn't acted uncomfortable. And he seemed to warm up to Nicholas right away. Of course, it was nearly impossible to avoid warming up to Nicholas if he wanted to be your friend. He could be a tad overwhelming, though.

But...I don't know. Having Jeremy join us was okay. We had some embarrassing moments, no doubt, but Jeremy...

well, he seems like a really nice person. And handsome. And kind of charming. Which only made her "getting a grip" condition more challenging.

Alison's heart ached again at the thought of Nicholas's comment. More than anything, she wished her son didn't have to experience so much grief so early in life. She wished he had Connor to play with and talk to and do things with. She wished she could have protected him from such a deep hurt.

She wished she could have protected them both, for that matter.

But nothing had protected her from losing her husband. She'd pleaded with God to heal Connor. She'd cried out in anguish again and again. She'd wept at the funeral and fallen to her knees.

And at the end of it all, she'd had to find the will to stand back up; the sight of a fearful five-year-old boy looking to her with tear-filled eyes had meant that somehow she would have to keep going. And so she did.

Despite her dismay at Nicholas's statement that having Jeremy join them was like having a dad, she completely understood what he meant. Just the presence of a man at the table with them reminded her of what life had been like with Connor.

It reminded her of how much she'd lost.

Chapter 3

The next morning Alison woke extra early, anxious about cooking breakfast for a well-established chef. Suddenly her meager supply of breakfast recipes seemed inadequate. But she knew better than to experiment with something new when serving guests. She and Connor had learned that the hard way. She smiled at the memory of the disastrous mushroom omelets they'd made one morning for a houseful of patrons. Connor had saved the day by rushing into town and coming back with a huge boxful of delicious doughnuts and pastries from the Donut Haus.

No, she'd stick with a tried and true recipe for Chef Jeremy. It might not be fancy, but at least she knew it inside and out. She shredded potatoes for hash browns, whipped up half a dozen eggs, chopped and seared cubes of ham and grated plenty of Swiss and cheddar cheese. She add some seasonings and cottage cheese, stirred the ingredients together, poured it into a dish and slid the casserole into the oven.

Soon the warm smell of breakfast filled the first floor of the house. The sun was just coming over the mountains as Alison arranged individual dishes of fresh fruit. She set out coffee, tea, orange juice, milk, slices of toast and glass jars with jam.

At eight o'clock on the dot, Jeremy came into the breakfast area dressed and ready for a day on the river. He set his fishing rod and gear by the back door and grabbed a plate at the end of the buffet table.

"This looks fantastic, but you didn't have to go to all this trouble for me, Alison. I know I'm the only guest. Really, if you set out a bowl of oatmeal, I'd be happy."

"Are you kidding? I want you to want to come back. And to go home and tell all your friends about the fantastic Mountain View B&B." Alison grinned.

"I can promise you I will. Won't you join me for breakfast? It seems like a shame to enjoy all this alone. Where's Nicholas?"

"He'll be up any minute. Yesterday's excitement must have worn him out." Alison filled her plate and they sat together at the breakfast table. Alison watched Jeremy close his eyes for a quick, silent prayer. She did the same. She'd sort of wished he had prayed aloud; she would have liked to hear him pray. As the two of them began to eat, Alison couldn't stop herself from feeling glad Jeremy had asked her to join him. It was so nice having another adult to eat with and talk to.

"I really like this casserole. I hope I can convince you to share the recipe with me," Jeremy said.

"Sure. I'm glad you like it. It's super easy to make, but don't tell anyone."

"Your secret is safe with me." Jeremy winked at her.

Alison felt a lump in her throat. It was an innocent comment, of course. But it had been so long since she'd had anyone to confide in.

"So, you're spending the day at the river, right?" Alison nodded toward the fishing gear. "I made you a sack lunch."

Jeremy looked surprised. "You didn't have to do that!"

"It was no trouble. Just a couple of turkey sandwiches."

"What are your plans for the day?" Jeremy asked.

"Nicholas and I will leave for church services once he's up. After that, we're having lunch with my parents. Then

I need to go to the grocery store. Also, the kitchen sink is leaking so I need to figure out what to do about that."

"I could help you," Jeremy offered. Alison shook her head.

"No, that's okay. I can handle it." Alison felt she had to refuse, but she wished she didn't have to, seeing as how she had about as much experience fixing leaks as she did teaching rocket science.

After a quiet moment, Alison plunged ahead. "By the way, thanks for being so understanding about Nicholas. I know he asks a lot of questions."

"There's nothing wrong with that. I really like him."

Alison looked down at her plate. "He's been through a lot. Losing his dad was really hard."

"I lost my dad five years ago and it was the hardest thing I've ever experienced. I can't imagine going through that as a child," Jeremy said softly. Alison looked up, surprised by Jeremy's candor. Without thinking, she reached over and squeezed his hand.

"I'm sorry you lost your dad," she said. "I wish I wasn't so familiar with loss, but I am, and I know it's painful."

"When did you lose your husband, Alison?" Jeremy asked, his voice filled with compassion. She withdrew her hand and looked back down at her plate.

"Two years ago," Alison tried to keep her voice stable. "Lymphoma. It was fast. He was fine…and we'd bought the B&B about a year before and things were going so well. Nicholas was five years old, precocious, funny—it was such a fun age. We were talking about having another baby. Then Connor went in for a checkup because he'd been feeling run-down and thought something was wrong. It was lymphoma, and he was gone in six months." Alison gasped for breath. She pushed the emotion—the unfairness of it all, the false sense that it was just a bad dream—down but it always surfaced again.

She couldn't breathe.

Connor.
I need you.

She gripped her napkin in her hand. Her whole body felt tight as she tried to breathe and hold back a flood of tears at the same time.

Jeremy reached over and took her hand.

"Alison," he said, his voice low and steady. "Alison," he repeated, and she forced her head up, gulping in a deep breath. "I'm so sorry that happened to you."

"Me too," Alison said, wiping away a tear that escaped.

After a good three hours of fishing, Jeremy felt ready to stop for lunch. The trout were rising and he couldn't have chosen a better spot for roll casting, but the sun was high and he knew he needed to eat. He found a nice flat rock to sit on and took out the sandwiches Alison had made for him. He couldn't stop thinking about their conversation over breakfast. Nicholas had come barreling into the kitchen after Alison had told Jeremy about her husband's death, so the exchange had come to a quick halt.

When a lone tear had trailed down Alison's face, Jeremy had fought the urge to reach over and wipe it away.

Why am I feeling so involved? I've barely met Alison, yet every time I'm around her, I feel captivated. Maybe it was just the intensity of the moment. They were both feeling emotional after talking about his dad and her husband.

She had been through so much. He couldn't even imagine losing a spouse like that. Now she was alone with a child to raise. And Nic…things would never be the same for either of them. *This trip hasn't started out as I expected.*

Jeremy finished his sandwiches and then walked downstream, taking a moment to switch flies before he continued fishing. The sun felt warm on his face, even as the occasional spray from the river chilled him. All in all, it was a fly fisherman's ideal day. But despite the solace of the river, heaviness permeated his spirit. He couldn't stop thinking of Alison, the way she'd gasped for breath and her white-knuckled grip on her napkin while she'd tried to hold herself together. The brokenness in her eyes when she'd finally looked up at him.

He hated to leave her feeling like that. He wished he could help lighten her load somehow.

Father, what's this about? I've been so busy the past few years that I haven't even dated, other than a few casual coffee dates. I've tried to avoid dating, actually. I'm not sure why. Maybe because it's hard to date when you're always working evenings. Then I come out here for some time alone on the river, and I can't stop thinking about the single mom I'm staying with.

Are you trying to tell me something?

A favorite Bible verse instantly came to mind. John 7:38. His mother had quoted it often back when he lived at home. *"The Lord will guide you always; he will satisfy your needs in a sun-scorched land and will strengthen your frame. You will be like a well-watered garden, like a spring whose waters never fail."*

The verse reached all the way to Jeremy's core. A sense that he was in the exact place where God wanted him settled over him.

Panic flooded through Alison as she looked over her bank statements later that afternoon. Once she and Nicholas had returned from the grocery store, she'd forced herself to log on to the computer to pay a few bills. Nicholas's college fund remained untouched, but as Alison watched her savings decrease as she withdrew money to cover the bills, she felt her chest tighten. If only she and Connor had known they wouldn't have years to rebuild their savings when they'd put every penny they had into the down payment for the house and the loan for renovations. If they'd had better insurance instead of being left with so many medical bills... If...if...if.

Father, what am I doing? I can't keep living like this. It's only a matter a time before that account runs dry. We don't have enough guests to come close to breaking even. Should I sell? I don't even know if I could sell right now. Maybe if I took a loss. I'd have to move in with Mom and Dad. I know they've offered over and over—but, Father, I want my own home with Nicholas. I want this *home. The home Connor and I made together. Nicholas would be absolutely heartbroken if we left this house. And so would I. How much more can I lose?*

Alison buried her head in her hands.

Oh God, please help.

Chapter 4

"Alison?"

Alison jolted and her head hit the pipe under the kitchen sink.

"Ouch!" She backed out from where she'd been kneeling on the floor.

"Everything okay?" Jeremy asked as he stood over her. Alison rubbed her head and grabbed the counter as she pulled herself up. She hadn't heard Jeremy come in through the back door. The late afternoon sun shone in through the window above the sink.

"Yeah. I just…I know there's a leak. So I was checking it out."

"Want me to take a look?"

"Oh no. Of course not. I'll just call a plumber." She bit her lip, thinking that maybe her dad could come over and help. Paying a plumber wasn't really what she needed at that moment.

"Move over and let me look, Alison," Jeremy said, unzipping his fishing vest and hanging it over one of the barstools. She hadn't seen him since he'd left for the river that Sunday morning. He moved past her, so close that their shoulders brushed.

"You don't have to," Alison protested as Jeremy bent down and stuck his head under the sink.

"It has a leak," he said after a few moments, his voice muffled.

Alison sighed. "I know." She waited, listening to Jeremy rummaging around in the cabinet. He finally backed out and stood facing her.

"I think I have good news for you."

Alison brightened. "Really?"

"The leak is in the hose. That can easily be replaced, and it's inexpensive."

Alison nodded. "That *is* good news. Thanks, Jeremy."

Easily replaced? Maybe for a plumber! I don't know the first thing about hoses and leaks.

Alison forced away those initial negative thoughts.

He said it's an easy fix. That's a relief. I'll figure out how to do it or I'll call my dad.

"Alison? Did you hear me?"

She blinked, lost in her thoughts. "Sorry. No. What did you say?"

"I just said the river was spectacular today. This is such a beautiful area."

Alison smiled. "It really is. How many fish did you catch?"

"Ten. I'm just planning to catch-and-release during this trip, though. Don't worry. I'm not going to stock your freezer with dead fish."

Alison chuckled. "That's a relief."

"It was a good day. Now I'm going to run into town for dinner."

Alison nodded, wishing he'd eat with her and Nicholas again. But she didn't feel like cooking, and there was absolutely no way she would invite Jeremy to eat store-bought pizza with them.

"How was church this morning?" Jeremy asked.

"Great. I've been going to River Community Church since I was a teenager, so it's like a second home to me. The people there are practically family to Nicholas and me."

Jeremy nodded. "I'd love to find one where I feel that way. I go to a really large church. I'm settled there and I like it for the most part, but a week doesn't go by where it seems I'm not asked if it's my first time attending. And I've been going there for about three years now."

Alison cocked her head to the side and nodded her understanding, all the while reminding herself that it probably wasn't appropriate to find Jeremy so appealing. He leaned against the counter, his demeanor a seemingly perfect blend of laid-back and serious. Alison smoothed back her ponytail, remembering that she'd just had her head in a cabinet and undoubtedly looked like a mess.

"So I'm going to head to town. Can I get you anything?"

Alison shook her head. "No, but thank you very much for asking. Maybe I'll see you when you get back."

"I hope so," Jeremy said. Alison swallowed with difficulty and stepped away from him.

"I'm going to go check on Nicholas. He had some homework to finish before Monday."

With one more step backward, she turned and left the kitchen.

Jeremy watched Alison retreat and stared at the empty kitchen doorframe for a moment. Then he got back on his hands and knees and disappeared under the cabinet again. He took down a few measurements and checked the size of the connections.

It's a good thing Dad taught me so many useful things. It helps to be something of a handyman.

Once he had the information he needed, Jeremy changed from his fishing attire to jeans and a sweatshirt and headed to Estes Park. He stopped at the hardware store first, and then dined on an unexceptional cheeseburger at a hole-in-the-wall restaurant on Main Street.

By the time he got home, night had fallen. He could hear voices in the basement, but the first floor was vacant. He poured himself a glass of water and read through a magazine at the kitchen table, rather hoping Alison or Nicholas would come upstairs. Before too long, Nicholas popped around the corner.

"Jeremy! You're here. Did you catch any fish today?" Jeremy couldn't help smiling back at the boy's animated face.

"I caught ten fish! Hey, do you know if your mom has any tools she uses for fixing things?"

Nicholas's head bobbed up and down. "Sure. My dad's toolbox. It's in the garage."

At the mention of Nicholas's dad, Jeremy felt concern. What if pulling out the tools upset Alison?

"Well, maybe I should just ask your mom. I wanted to try to fix the leak under the sink."

"Can I help?" Nicholas eyes danced with hopefulness and Jeremy couldn't say no.

"Sure. But about the tools—"

"I'll go get my dad's toolbox. Mom won't mind, I'm sure." Nicholas took off toward the front door.

I'm not so sure she won't mind.

Alison entered the kitchen just as Nicholas came crashing through the front door carrying a bulging toolbox with both hands.

"Mom! Jeremy's going to fix the leak in the kitchen. He said I could help! Isn't that great?"

Her line of sight went from the toolbox to Jeremy, and Jeremy's stomach flip-flopped. He held up the plastic bag from the hardware store.

"I picked up a hose and a few other things," he admitted sheepishly. "I hope that's okay, Alison. Nic asked if he could help. . ."

"I see. Um, that's fine, I guess. Thank you."

"Here are my dad's tools!" With a huff, Nicholas set the toolbox on the table, and Jeremy winced at the sound. He hoped Alison really didn't mind. He just wanted to help her.

"I think I'll sit out here in the living room while you guys work on the leak. Okay, Nic?"

"Sure! We'll have this fixed in no time. Right, Jeremy?"

Jeremy noticed that Alison didn't make eye contact with him. "I hope so, buddy. Let's get to work."

Half an hour later, Nicholas helped Jeremy clean up the mess and put back the tools. As he turned the water to the house back on, Jeremy tried to keep up with Nicholas's steady chatter. The boy had asked question after question through every step of the plumbing process. Jeremy hadn't minded. He didn't normally spend very much time around kids, but he'd always wanted his own. And from what he could tell, Nicholas was a great kid—protective of his mother, happy to help, lonely for his father.

"Well? What's the verdict?" Jeremy looked up to see Alison leaning against the doorway, her arms crossed but her voice cheerful.

"We fixed it, Mom! Jeremy knew just what to do, and he showed me and so I helped him."

She focused on Nicholas. "That's so great, Nic. Thank you for helping." Her gaze lifted to Jeremy. "And thank you, Jeremy. You really didn't have to do this."

Jeremy shrugged. "I wanted to, Alison. It's not a big deal. I'm glad I could help."

She just looked at him for a moment. "Well, you've helped me a lot and I appreciate it. Now, Nic, it's time to wash up and get ready for bed."

"But, Mom—"

"No 'buts.' You have school tomorrow. Say good-night to Jeremy and head downstairs."

"All right," Nic said. "Good night, Jeremy."

Jeremy grinned. "Good night, buddy. I'll see you tomorrow, okay?"

At the sound of that, Nic brightened. He nodded. "Sure! I'll see you!" then he took off toward the basement stairs.

"Thanks again for your help," Alison said, her voice just a little softer. "So you said you were a chef. Where do these handyman skills come from?"

Jeremy set the toolbox on the counter. "My dad. He was in the Air Force when I was younger, but by the time I was in middle school he'd gotten out and worked in construction. I worked with him sometimes when I was in high school. A few things stuck, I guess."

She tilted her head to the side. "I wondered if you came from a military family."

"Really? What gave me away?"

Alison smiled. "The haircut. And your posture." Then her voice took on a serious note. "You'll let me know if Nic becomes a bother, right?"

"He's not a bother to me, Alison," Jeremy assured her. "In fact, I was thinking maybe he could fish with me after school… You could come too, of course. Or we could stay right in the line of sight from the house." Jeremy stopped talking and watched Alison digest his words. She seemed unsure and he felt ridiculous for even bringing it up.

"It's an open invitation, so just think about it," he said, hoping to smooth over the awkward moment.

"Okay," she said slowly. "I'll think about it. Don't mention it to Nic, okay? He'll jump on the idea. I'll let you know what I decide."

"Absolutely."

"If you want, you could have dinner with us tomorrow. My way of saying 'thank you' for fixing the leak." Her gaze dropped to the floor, and Jeremy had a feeling she wasn't altogether comfortable with her own offer. Still, maybe it would help keep her from feeling like she owed him anything.

He smiled at her. "Sure. Dinner would be nice."

Chapter 5

Monday morning Alison set out a traditional breakfast for Jeremy—scrambled eggs, bacon and pancakes—then took Nicholas to school. After dropping him off, she drove to the bank with a sense of dread. Mark Harmen, the banker she and Connor had worked with since the purchase of the B&B, was a Christian man, and Alison knew he sympathized with her situation. She also knew him to be honest and straightforward, so she'd called and asked for a meeting to go over her financial situation.

She sat nervously across from him in a plush leather chair and tried not to bite her nails as he reviewed her statements.

"Okay," Mark said after a few moments. As he folded his hands on the table, a memory flashed through Alison's mind. She and Connor were seated in the same room across from Mark, waiting anxiously to see if they would be approved for the loan for the B&B. She remembered Connor reaching over and taking her hand tightly in his.

Now she sat alone. No one could help ease the anxiety. The empty chair next to her felt like a stinging splash of cold water. A stark picture of her life. How could everything have changed so much in just a few short years?

You're not alone.

She took an unsteady breath and bowed her head for a moment.

Father, I need you. I need you to be my husband, my

savior, my friend, my adviser. I need you to please help me to know what to do.

She opened her eyes and looked at Mark, who was waiting patiently. She felt he probably knew she had been praying.

"Alison, the bottom line is that if things don't pick up soon with the B&B, financially it would be a mistake to continue with it. You have to think of your future. Of your son's future. You could, of course, continue to supplement your income with Connor's life insurance money. We've set aside money for Nicholas's college fund, and as you have wisely decided, we won't be touching that. The rest is up to your discretion. But over the course of the past two years, the B&B hasn't come close to breaking even, as you know."

Alison nodded. "I know. But I don't want to give up yet." The words came out in a whisper, so she cleared her throat and tried to seem more confident.

Mark's face was full of understanding. "I suggest you pray about this, Alison. I support your decision no matter what. But maybe it's time to give yourself a timetable. Such as, if things don't pick up in six months, it may be time to think about selling and downsizing. That sort of thing. I know things are tight for you, but for the B&B to succeed, you need to brainstorm ways to make that happen. Something has to change because you're not suddenly going to be flooded with guests. Meanwhile, you're losing money— significantly—every month. But, you could sell and buy a smaller place in town. Just think about it, Alison."

Mark's comments followed her long after the meeting had ended, along with the clear realization that selling didn't necessarily mean moving in with her parents. She'd made it on her own for two years without Connor. She could buy a small home in town and find a job. It would still mean losing the B&B, but she'd be able to maintain a home for herself and Nic.

Alison parked in town and walked to Starbucks, where

she was meeting her best friend, Michelle, for coffee. Alison felt that she and Michelle, both being single moms of eight-year-old sons, had a special heart connection.

With skin the color of dark cocoa and a smile that could encourage anyone, Michelle's inner beauty only enhanced her outer beauty. She managed a local hair salon and led a women's Bible study at River Community Church.

Michelle was waiting outside, and she held out a coffee cup to Alison. "Pumpkin spice latte. They've started with the fall flavors and I knew you'd want one."

"You shouldn't have! But thank you. I'm treating you next time," Alison said, warming her hands around the cup. "Let's walk. I love the brisk air."

Michelle nodded. "I know. I just love autumn in the mountains."

The two women walked down the sidewalk, chatting easily. Both women stopped at the sight of a large sign being hung over the street.

"The fall festival is next week? Already?" Alison said, surprised.

"Yes. They're having it the last weekend in September. I think that's actually a little earlier than last year. The church will have a booth. What about you? Were you thinking of getting a booth for the B&B?"

"I can't afford one. I think the registration is seven hundred dollars or something like that. But I just hadn't realized that it's already happening. I look forward to the festival every year. I guess I've been preoccupied with having a guest in the house. Time is getting away from me."

"You know, it would be a shame for your guest to leave right before the festival. It starts next Thursday. You should tell him about it."

"I'm sure he has to get back to his job. Did I tell you that my visitor is a chef who likes to fly-fish in his spare time? And he's so nice. He fixed the leak under my kitchen sink!"

"Really? That's pretty great," Michelle said. They kept

walking slowly, in time to see another sign going up about the festival's chili cook-off. Alison paused to read the sign.

$50 registration fee and $500 prize, including free marketing opportunities

Mark Harmen's voice invaded Alison's consciousness. *Brainstorm ideas.*

Michelle was reading the sign alongside her and obviously came to the same conclusion.

"How's your chili recipe?" she asked.

"Probably not worth five hundred dollars," she said, her voice laced with discouragement.

"Too bad there's not a chef around when you need one," Michelle said with a dramatic sigh.

Alison shook her head. "Oh, I couldn't ask Jeremy to help me."

"Jeremy, huh? Well, why not? If the man's willing to climb under your sink and fix a leak, I'm sure he's willing to help you perfect your chili recipe."

"But do you think that's fair? I mean, he's a gourmet chef. Would it be cheating to have him help me?"

"You could put his name on the ballot next to yours as co-chefs. Then offer to split the money with him if you win. Two hundred and fifty dollars may not be a lot, but the free marketing would be great, Alison."

"True," Alison murmured. "Maybe I'll ask him." She sipped her latte and felt the cool air whip her hair. She and Michelle sat down on a bench together.

"How's Shawn doing?" Alison asked. Michelle looked out at the mountain scene in front of them. From nearly every spot in the small town, a person could look up and enjoy the picturesque view.

"He's okay. He loves school and playing soccer. But it was just decided that he'll be going to his dad's for Thanksgiving. I'm a little sad about that."

Alison squeezed Michelle's arm. "Does that mean you have him for Christmas?"

Michelle gave her a small smile. "Yes, that's the plan. At least I have him for Christmas."

Alison understood Michelle's sadness. A few years before, Michelle's husband had left her and Shawn for another woman. He'd moved to Denver, where his pregnant girlfriend lived, and married her soon after she'd given birth to their child. Shawn had been devastated by his father's absence. Now he rarely saw him except for holidays and a few weeks during the summer.

Alison knew that the broken marriage had shattered Michelle, but seeing her son's pain and being away from him hurt her on a whole different level.

"Does Shawn know he's spending Thanksgiving with his dad?" Alison asked.

Michelle nodded. "Sure. We talked through everything. I think he wants to see his dad, but he's always sad to leave me alone. And despite the fact that I try to be positive about his time with his father, I think sometimes Shawn feels he has to contain his excitement so he doesn't hurt my feelings. We're still working on that. To be completely honest, my feelings can get hurt. But I *never* want that to come across to Shawn. It's a battle to stay positive sometimes, but my little boy's feelings are worth the effort," Michelle said with determination.

"And you won't be alone on Thanksgiving, Michelle. You'll be at my house. Unless you have other plans."

Michelle smiled. "I know there's always a place for me. God's been so good to me to give me a church family like River Community. I'm thinking of taking the holiday to drive down to see my parents in Colorado Springs, but if that changes, I'll be at your table," Michelle promised. "You know, Ali, if you're going to sign up for the chili cook-off, you'll need to do it soon."

"I know," Alison agreed. "I'll think about it. It sounds… fun," Alison said. Michelle nudged her shoulder.

"It's okay to have fun, Alison. You know that, right? It's *okay*."

Alison knew Michelle understood how conflicted her emotions could get when it came to enjoying any part of life, other than Nic, after losing Connor. But in her heart, where she still held him close, Alison could almost see Connor and hear his jovial voice telling her, *Yeah, Ali. It's okay to have fun.*

The thought comforted her, yet caused her heart to ache at the same time.

Chapter 6

After their coffee date, Alison and Michelle drove over to the church. While Wednesday was to be the kickoff for the fall soup kitchen, some of the helpers were getting together to prepare sandwiches ahead of time. Alison walked into the kitchen, where a handful of women of varying ages were putting together platters of cold-cut sandwiches. Alison washed her hands and took a spot in the assembly line.

Mary Margaret Olson, one of Alison's close friends, acknowledged her presence with a welcoming smile and then passed a plate of sliced cheeses down the line. "Your mother was here earlier dropping off a few cakes for lunch Wednesday. She told us you have a guest this week. That's great!"

Alison sighed and placed a slice of provolone on one side of a sub sandwich. "I suppose. But it would take a whole lot of guests to make up the difference in my finances this month."

Mary looked at her sympathetically. "It'll pick up soon."

"I hope," Alison answered. "So how many sandwiches are we making?"

"As many as possible," Cori, another good friend of Alison's, said. "We're making two platters of ham sandwiches, two platters of turkey, one of roast beef, one of chicken salad and one of tuna. We're also going to have at least three big pots of tortilla soup and bread to serve. Karen and Mark and James and Sonya signed up to come in Wednesday morning to make the soup. Like I said, your mom brought in two chocolate cakes this morning. Amelia Delaney will drop off two vanilla cakes tomorrow, and Mary Margaret, here, brought an extra chocolate today.

"Like last year, we'll be serving lunch on Wednesdays and dinner on Fridays. Plus we'll have brown bags with snacks available on Mondays. The doors open to the public the day after tomorrow and I have a feeling we're going to have a big crowd for lunch. With the weather turning a little chilly, people are thankful for a warm meal."

Murmurs of agreement filled the kitchen. It was one of the things Alison loved about their church, the deep-rooted heart to help out the less fortunate in their small, tourist town. For such a small area, the number of homeless people astounded Alison.

The previous year the congregation had unanimously agreed to open a soup kitchen. And helping out ministered to Alison's soul. A few hours of concentrating on helping others helped her refocus her perspective on the positives in her life—like Nicholas and her family. And to be honest, she was getting to the point where she was just a few paychecks from needing a soup line herself. All the more reason to help.

Alison listened to the streams of conversation around her as she put sandwiches together. These same women had stocked her freezer with meals when Connor died. They'd come by to help clean house when she could barely leave her bedroom. They'd helped shuttle Nicholas back and forth to school functions. Along with her parents, the women in this room had made all the difference in bringing Alison back to life when she'd felt sure her life was over.

"So tell us about your mystery guest," Lenora Santiago, a woman Alison's mother's age and someone Alison considered one of the kindest women she knew, asked. Alison exchanged a quick glance with Michelle, who was farther down near the end of the line.

Every eye was on Alison and she cleared her throat. "No mystery there. Just a fisherman who came up from the city to fish for a week. Well, he's sort of a fisherman. He's also a chef."

"A chef! Wow! We should have enlisted him to make the soup," Mary Margaret joked.

"He works for Romano's in downtown Denver," Alison told them.

"I've eaten there before!" Mary Margaret exclaimed. "That's a fantastic restaurant. If he decides to do any cooking at your house, Alison, you better call me. I can accidentally stop by around dinnertime."

Alison laughed. "I'm supposed to be serving him, remember? Which is highly unfortunate because my cooking skills are not worth talking about."

"Not true," Lenora said with a shake of her head. "We can't all be chefs, can we? Besides, you only have to cook him breakfast. That's not so difficult."

"Well, um," Alison began and the room fell silent. She hoped she wasn't blushing. "He ended up eating spaghetti with Nic and me the other night. And then he fixed the leak under the kitchen sink for me, so I invited him to have dinner with us again tonight."

Surprised smiles filled the faces of the women around her, and Alison wanted to roll her eyes.

"Oh, really?" Mary Margaret said with a sly grin.

"Don't go there. It's nothing. And don't put more pressure on me. I'm nervous enough about cooking for a well-established chef tonight without you ladies making a big deal about it."

"What are you making?" Lenora asked.

"Nothing fancy. Pork chops with twice-baked potatoes and an apple pie for dessert."

"That sounds delicious. I'm looking forward to apple picking this fall," Mary Margaret said wistfully.

Alison was thankful the conversation had steered away

from her fisherman/chef guest. As the women shared their favorite apple recipes she moved to help Michelle make tuna sandwiches.

"So?" Michelle raised her eyebrows.

"So what?"

"You didn't mention that you'd asked him to have dinner with you and Nic! I think you'd better tell me more about Jeremy. What's he like?"

Alison sighed and scooped a spoonful of the tuna, pickle and mayo mixture onto a slice of wheat bread.

"He's attractive—I'm not going to lie. And he's friendly. He's a believer, too. Nicholas has latched onto him like butter on toast."

Michelle smiled at the pun, but Alison saw concern in the way her eyebrows furrowed. "Are you okay with that?"

"I don't know. Of course, I understand Nic's desire to have a man to do things with. He misses his dad. But I don't want him to be brokenhearted when Jeremy leaves in a week."

"I understand how you feel. If you think that Nic is becoming a little too enthralled with Jeremy, call me. I could always take Nic for a night or two. He and Shawn play together so well."

Alison truly appreciated the offer. "Thanks, Michelle. I'll keep that in mind."

"You'd better get out of here early. If it were me cooking for a chef, I'd want plenty of time to get dinner on the table. Especially a cute chef," Michelle said playfully.

In spite of herself, a smile inched up on Alison's face.

Jeremy carefully stepped further into the rushing water, thankful he had his waders, knowing how cold the water must be. A strong breeze brushed past his face and rustled the trees lining the river, causing a sound almost like that of applause to fill the area. He cast his fly rod and watched the line land as light as a feather on the water.

Although he enjoyed the solitude of the river, Jeremy appreciated the sounds around him—the rippling water, the yellow leaves dancing with the breeze, birds calling. He inhaled the cool air deeply and felt a slight tug on his line. He snapped the line back, his attention directed to the trout.

Once he'd secured the fish, taking note of its weight and length and lovely color, he released the fish back into the water. As he bent to choose another fly to fish with, his mind drifted to Alison's dinner.

Despite Alison's obvious hesitation, Jeremy was glad for the invitation. As much as he was enjoying every moment spent on the river, he'd checked his watch more than once, anxious for dinner. Alison had set out sandwiches again for him and Jeremy hoped she knew how much he appreciated the gesture. He wished he could contribute to the evening meal somehow, but he didn't feel that was an option at this point.

A few hours later, he stomped his boots on the back porch, trying to dislodge any mud before trekking through the house. He opened the back door and stepped inside. The smells of pork and apple pie wafted through the house, but Jeremy didn't see Alison anywhere. Nicholas sat at the dining room table, working on homework. He looked up and his whole face brightened at the sight of Jeremy.

"Jeremy! How was fishing today?"

"Excellent," Jeremy leaned over one of the chairs at the table. "The weather was perfect and the fish were biting. How was school?"

"Good. We had a substitute. She let us play spelling games."

"Almost finished, Nic?"

Jeremy looked up as Alison walked into the room. In jeans and a pink T-shirt, with her blond hair tied into an intricate braid over her right shoulder, she looked prettier than ever. Jeremy cleared his throat.

What had gotten into him? *I'd better take it down a*

notch. It's like I have a high school crush on this woman!
She's a single mom who misses her husband and is trying
to run a business. What am I thinking?

Nicholas slammed his book closed. "All done, Mom!"

"Great. Then can you set the table for us?"

"I'm going to go upstairs and clean up, if there's time,"
Jeremy said. Alison nodded, just barely making eye contact with him.

"Of course. Go ahead," she told him. "Oh…um, I hope
you like pork chops," she said nervously. Jeremy gave her
an easy smile.

"I do. Very much. Again, thanks for inviting me to join
you guys."

"It's the least we could do after you replaced the hose
and everything."

Jeremy shrugged. "Not a problem. I'll be back downstairs shortly," he said as he headed upstairs. He took a fast
shower, deciding at the last minute to shave. He wanted to
appear a little less rough around the edges at dinner.

Why did he feel nervous? It was pretty obvious he'd neglected his social life to the point where eating pork chops
at a B&B in the mountains with a nice woman and an eight-
year-old boy felt like a date. *Maybe I need to get out more*
when I'm back in Denver.

"Jeremy, you can sit here," Nicholas pulled out a chair
as Jeremy approached the table.

"Thanks, buddy. I'm excited to try your mom's pork
chops."

"She's a really good cook," Nicholas stated proudly.
Walking up behind Nic, Alison blushed. She shook her
head at Jeremy and mouthed, "Not really." Jeremy just
winked at her.

They all sat down to eat and Alison prayed over their
meal. Nicholas sparked the conversation by telling Jeremy
all about a stray cat that seemed to have adopted his grandparents. That story led to Alison giving Jeremy a little more

information about her parents. Jeremy could tell that they were a very active part of Alison and Nicholas's life there in Estes Park. By the end of the meal, Jeremy and Alison were both in stitches over Nicholas's imitation of his grandfather's frustration over the stubborn cat.

As the conversation wound down, Alison glanced at Nicholas, then rested her chin on her folded hands. "So, Jeremy, would tomorrow afternoon be a good time to show Nic the ropes when it comes to fly-fishing?"

Nicholas's eyes widened like saucers, and his mouth dropped open before it closed in an ear-to-ear grin.

Jeremy set down his napkin and nodded. "Tomorrow would be great. What do you say, Nic? Want to learn to fly-fish?"

Nicholas almost jumped out of his seat. "Yes! Totally. Yes. But I don't have a fly rod," he said as an afterthought, his face falling.

"Oh, don't worry about that. I have an extra. Will you come with us, Alison?" Jeremy asked, hope in his voice. Alison's gaze met his and Jeremy held his breath.

I'm not doing a very good job of taking it down a notch.

"We'll see," Alison said with a smile.

Chapter 7

Late Tuesday afternoon, Alison stood on the deck watching the guys prepare to fish. Jeremy and Nic were both hunched down by the water looking through Jeremy's reserve of flies. She could see Nic asking questions and Jeremy explaining to him the process of fly-fishing. Alison enjoyed seeing how thoughtfully Nic was taking every instruction. Both Jeremy and Nic were taking the lesson very seriously.

Nic touched his lips and then leaned forward to point at something, and Alison froze for a moment. They were identical to her own gestures. Even from a distance, she could see Nic's furrowed brow as he tried to grasp the gist of what Jeremy was saying. That furrowed brow and intent look—so like her.

The picture stunned her.

She liked to see Connor in Nicholas. She always looked for similarities between the two of them. So much so that she'd neglected to see herself in her son. That thoughtful, intentional side of Nic was all Alison. If people ever told her that Nic reminded them of her, Alison was quick to say he was just like his father. And in many ways, especially his dark eyes and dark hair, Nic did favor Connor. But watching him now, Alison soaked in the truth.

My son is like his mother. He's a perfect blend of me and Connor, but he's very much like me.

She held that thought and tried to decipher what feelings

it evoked in her. Looking out at her son as he practiced roll casting with Jeremy, she only felt a surge of love and pride.

Alison sighed and moved to the kitchen sink to wash her hands. It was meatloaf night, and at this point, she just assumed that Jeremy would join them. After school, Nicholas had changed in record speed and, with barely a nod to Alison, burst out the back door where Jeremy was waiting for him. Alison appreciated that even without her instruction, Jeremy made sure they stayed right in the line of view from the house. From where she worked in the kitchen, she could see the guys practicing casting.

As she chopped onions and added them to the meatloaf mixture, Alison thought over the implications of asking Jeremy to help her with the chili cook-off.

I shouldn't involve him. It's not fair to him, really. He's planning to leave Saturday and he might feel like he has to stay to help me.

Then again, we could spend some time cooking before he plans to leave, and I can still enter his name alongside mine if he's not here. And in the unlikely event we win, I can send him his share of the prize money.

Alison added more salt and pepper, then deemed the mixture ready. She transferred it to a baking pan and slid it into the oven, then pulled ingredients from the refrigerator to make a simple chopped salad. With a side glance, she could see Nicholas and Jeremy laughing. The sight brought an automatic smile to Alison's face.

Once she could smell the meatloaf cooking and the salad sat ready in the refrigerator, Alison slid on her boots and walked down to the river.

"Mom! Watch!" Nicholas yelled gleefully from a few feet down the river. Alison clapped as he cast the line out onto the water.

"Great job!" she called out. Jeremy moved to stand next to her.

"He's a natural," Jeremy told her. "And I'm afraid to tell you that I think he's hooked on fly-fishing."

Alison shrugged. "I'm not surprised. The river is in Nic's blood. He's been fishing with my dad several times, but fly-fishing is new to him. I'm glad he likes it."

"He certainly lives in the perfect spot for it," Jeremy said as they both watched Nicholas. Alison's chest tightened just a bit at the ever-present reality that Nicholas might not live by a river for much longer.

"By the way, it's meatloaf night and I hope you'll join us, Jeremy." Alison looked over at him.

"I hate to intrude again, Alison. I feel like I should pay you extra for all these meals!"

Alison waved off the comment. "Are you kidding? You've fixed my kitchen sink and taught my son to fly-fish—I think you deserve a plate of meatloaf on the house."

Jeremy chuckled. "Well, I'll take you up on the offer. Thank you."

"And speaking of things you've done for me…I have a favor to ask," Alison began. Jeremy gave her his full attention.

"You probably didn't know this, but our annual Estes Park Fall Festival is next week. It's a great event with lots of booths and fun activities. Anyway, there's a chili cook-off this year. I wasn't even thinking of entering—but the winner gets $500 and free marketing opportunities. My chili recipe isn't really award-worthy, so I wondered if you could give me some ideas to shake up the recipe. I'd enter both our names, and if we win, I'll split the prize money with you, of course," Alison finished.

Jeremy stroked his chin and didn't answer for a moment, during which time Alison began to feel like an idiot for even asking.

"When is the festival?" he asked.

That wasn't exactly the enthusiastic response Alison had hoped for, but she swallowed her feelings.

Why on earth did I ask?

"It starts next Thursday and goes through the weekend. I think the chili cook-off is Friday, though."

Jeremy was still quiet.

"You absolutely don't have to stay longer. I was just thinking if you could give me some tips to improve my recipe…"

"I'd love to stay for the festival, actually. But I'll need to call my boss and see if that's even an option," Jeremy responded.

Alison paused, trying to temper down the uncontrolled rise of excitement she suddenly felt. "You would?"

Jeremy nodded. "Sure, it sounds like a lot of fun. And my go-to chili recipe might not be award-worthy either, but I've got a buddy who owns a café in downtown Denver and makes top-of-the-line chili. He's a firefighter and a chef, and practically every firefighter in the city swears his chili is the best. So I'll call Ethan and ask him for some recommendations on spices. We'll need to practice until we know we've got it right."

We.

"Mom, did you see that?!"

Alison's attention diverted to where Nicholas was leaning in to look at something in the river.

"Nic, be careful!" Alison's shout caused her son to jolt, and he stumbled closer to the water. In a flash, Jeremy was behind Nicholas, pulling him back.

"Careful, buddy," Jeremy said as he made sure Nic was secure on the riverbank. Alison jumped to Nic's side. She bit back the scolding that was right behind her teeth once she saw the look on his face.

"Sorry, Mom. But I saw this really cool turtle in the water. I'm okay, though." Nicholas put his arms around her waist; she could hear in his voice that he knew he'd scared her.

And he had. Even the thought of anything happening to

Nicholas caused Alison's heart rate to triple. She hugged Nicholas back tightly while planting a kiss on the top of his head.

"It's okay. Just be careful," she managed to say.

"Should we pack up and go in?" Jeremy asked. Alison looked at a crestfallen Nicholas and shook her head.

"No, it's fine. Nic will be careful. I'm going to go check on our meatloaf. You guys stay here and keep fishing. I'll ring the bell when dinner's ready, which should be soon."

Nicholas hugged his mom again. "Thanks, Mom!"

"I'll watch him," Jeremy said, looking right at Alison so she knew he meant it. She peered at those kind hazel eyes of his.

"I know you will."

Jeremy watched Alison head back to the house, then helped Nicholas choose a new fly and patiently showed him again how to tie it to the line. He'd felt almost as panicked as Alison had seemed at the sight of Nicholas stumbling toward the water.

He understood her fear. Nicholas was her whole world. Jeremy watched him closely as they fished.

"My mom really worries about me," Nicholas explained after a while.

"Of course she does. She's your mom," Jeremy said.

"No, it's not just that. It's because of my dad."

The boy's voice was quiet and Jeremy's heart tugged.

"She's a little better now. She used to cry all the time. She tried not to let me see, but I could hear her. Sometimes she still cries but not as much. I'm glad. It made me really sad, too, whenever she cried."

Jeremy wished he knew the right words to say. He knew he needed to say *something*. Nicholas was confiding in him, after all.

"My dad passed away, too," Jeremy said, working hard to steady his voice. Nicholas looked at him with big eyes.

"Really? I'm sorry for you."

Jeremy nodded. "Thanks, Nic. I miss him a lot. But he's part of who I am. Just like your dad is part of who you are. He'll always be part of you. I'm sure there are things about you that are just like your dad."

Nicholas nodded slowly. "My hair and my eyes are like his. And pizza is my favorite food, too. And he and I both liked comic books. And we liked video games."

Jeremy smiled. "I have the same color hair as my dad, too. And he and I both liked to fish. We used to fish together sometimes."

"My mom says it's okay to talk about my dad whenever I want to. But I think sometimes it makes her sad."

"She misses him. But she has you, Nicholas. And that makes her happy. *You* make her happy."

Nicholas looked at the river and thought this over.

"I do make her happy," he concluded. Jeremy patted him on the shoulder.

"Of course you do, Nic."

"But I think she needs more than just me." Nicholas cast his line.

"Is that right?" Jeremy asked, his voice even and curious.

"Yeah, I think so."

"How do you feel about that? About her maybe needing more than just you?"

Nicholas was quiet for a long moment, with only the sound of the fast water filling their ears. Jeremy was content to wait.

"I don't know," Nicholas finally broke the silence. "I guess it depends on who the other person is."

Jeremy nodded, casting his line again. "That seems like a fair judgment to me."

"I want her to be happy."

"I'm sure you do," Jeremy said.

"I miss having a dad. Most of the other kids at school

have one. My dad was a good dad. We did a lot of stuff together."

"No one will ever replace your dad, Nic. For you or your mom."

"Do you think Mom will ever want another husband, though?" Nic's voice dropped a notch; he sounded a bit uneasy.

Jeremy again wondered how he'd found himself in a situation where he was having this kind of conversation. It certainly wasn't how he'd pictured his vacation.

He pulled back his line to change his fly. "Have you asked her?"

Nicholas sighed. "Yes. I asked her one time. She said, 'I doubt it.' Then she said, 'Let's talk about something else.'"

"I see. Things would change for you guys if she married someone, Nic. Do you think you'd be okay with that?"

Nicholas looked sideways at Jeremy.

"Maybe."

Chapter 8

"Are you sure it's not too much of an inconvenience?" Jeremy asked his boss, Leo Romano. He paced in his bedroom upstairs, cell phone to his ear. After the fishing lesson, he'd eaten dinner with Alison and Nicholas, then excused himself to go upstairs and make a few calls.

"Jeremy, it's not a problem. You have plenty of vacation time. I'll be in town, so I can easily cover your shift if Margo isn't available or if we're shorthanded. It's fine for you to take another week. This is your first vacation in...I can't even remember how long! Have you ever taken a vacation before?" Leo laughed and Jeremy chuckled with him.

"All right, all right. If you're sure. Put me on the schedule for the following Sunday night. I'll either leave next Saturday or Sunday morning. Either way, I'll be back in Denver in plenty of time to be at Romano's that evening. I might even make it for Saturday night. If that's the case, I'll give you as much notice as possible."

"Will do. That works for me. How are things going up there? Are you catching any fish? Enjoying the solitude?"

Jeremy smiled to himself. *Solitude* wasn't exactly the word he'd use to describe his experience up to this point. And he didn't mind a bit.

"It's going really well. I love being up here in the mountains. And I'm at a great place for fishing."

"Well, I'm glad you're enjoying yourself. Don't worry

about Romano's. We'll handle everything until you're back in the kitchen."

Jeremy said goodbye and then found Ethan Carter's name in his contacts. Ethan was married to Leo's sister, Isabella, and over the past year, Jeremy had become good friends with him. Jeremy enjoyed the entire Romano family, to be honest. They were welcoming people and often included him in their family gatherings.

Ethan answered right away, and the two men talked shop as it applied to chili recipes. Jeremy could hear Isabella calling out suggestions in the background. He could also hear the wail of Ethan and Isabella's newborn daughter, Layla. Jeremy took notes as Ethan listed the best spices to use.

"So, you're staying with a single mom and her son?" Ethan asked.

"Well…yes. I mean, I'm renting a room at Alison's B&B."

"Alison?"

Jeremy had a feeling he knew where the conversation was leading.

"Yes, her name is Alison," he said, making sure to keep his voice indifferent. He could hear muffled sounds as Ethan talked to Isabella.

"Isa wants to know if you think Alison's pretty," Ethan said with a snicker.

"Tell Isa not to worry about it," Jeremy quipped back. Ethan laughed out loud.

"So…that's a yes," he surmised.

"I'll let you guys know how the chili turns out," Jeremy said.

"Sure. Hey, wait!" Muffled sounds again. "Okay, Isa said to tell you that romance starts in the kitchen."

"She knows this from experience, I presume?" Jeremy said with a roll of his eyes.

"We both do," Ethan answered.

"Moving on. I've got to go. I'll call you if I need help—in the kitchen, *not* the romance department!" Jeremy hung up the phone. He didn't mind the jesting. If the truth were told, he appreciated having people in his life who cared enough to inquire.

He slipped his phone into his back pocket and headed downstairs to give Alison the good news that she had a partner for the chili cook-off.

When he got to the kitchen, he found Nicholas at the table doing his homework and Alison loading the dishwasher.

"So, when can we go shopping for ingredients? I've got a list of spices we need to pick up," Jeremy said, folding his arms and leaning against the kitchen counter. Nicholas and Alison looked up with surprise. A smile spread across Alison's face.

"Really? We're entering the cook-off!"

"Entering? We're in it to win it, my friend," Jeremy announced, and both Nicholas and Alison laughed.

Nicholas jumped up. "Hey! Does that mean you're staying longer?"

"It sure does. I'll be here till after the cook-off."

Nicholas let out a whoop. "Isn't that awesome, Mom? Jeremy's staying longer! And he's going to the festival with us!"

Jeremy watched Alison's reaction. She cocked her head to the side and grinned at him. He could see she was pleased.

"It *is* awesome," she said warmly.

While Nicholas packed up his homework, Jeremy moved to talk with Alison where Nicholas couldn't hear their conversation.

"Just to clarify, Alison, of course I'll be paying to stay here next week also."

She looked torn. "I hate for you to do that. It was my idea, after all."

He shook his head and kept his voice low. "I insist. And honestly, it's been a really long time since I've had a vacation. I could use the time away from work. Being up here in the mountains and by the river has been good for me. I cleared it with my boss and he assured me he can spare me for another week. And besides, I'm hoping I'll get another taste of that breakfast casserole you made. I really do want the recipe."

Alison smiled; it reached her eyes and made them sparkle.

Something about the fact that he was the one who put that sparkle in her eyes made Jeremy feel gratified.

Long after the house was dark and quiet, he lay awake, thinking about Alison.

I've been here five days. Just five days. And I'm not sure I can ignore the fact that I really like this woman. She's been dealt more than I can imagine, and she keeps going. She's fierce when it comes to loving Nicholas. I admire her. I'll admit it—I wonder if she could love anyone else as much as she does her son. I wonder if she'll ever have room in her heart to let go of Connor and move on.

But I've got to keep a hold of these crazy feelings. I would never want to hurt Alison. I'd never want to lead her on. And I'd certainly never want to hurt Nicholas. He misses having his dad in his life. And the plain truth is that I'll be here for a few more days, then I go back to my life in Denver. I can't get so emotionally involved. But if Ethan and Isa are right and romance does *start in the kitchen… I've just put myself in a precarious spot. Because that's just where we'll be until the festival.*

Alison tossed and turned in her bed. She kept thinking about the excitement in Jeremy's face as he'd talked about entering the cook-off together…and Nicholas's obvious elation that Jeremy would be staying. Nicholas and Jeremy seemed to have quickly developed a comfortable friendship. Although Alison worried that Nicholas would be overly disappointed when Jeremy left, she also appreciated that Jeremy included Nicholas. Plans for attending the festival and entering the cook-off had consumed all conversation until Alison had insisted it was bedtime for Nicholas.

With a frustrated huff, she blew her hair from her face and kicked off the covers tangled around her legs. She stared at the ceiling, a prayer forming in her heart.

Seriously, Father? The first guest you send me in a month is a good-looking single guy who just happens to be great with my son? I can't do this! My heart was already dangerously close to the edge, and now Jeremy's staying another whole week! Don't get me wrong—the thought of him leaving makes me just as overwhelmed. But I have too much going on in my life to dissolve into this crush every time I'm with him. I have my financial mess. I don't think I'm ready to move on from loving Connor. And I have Nicholas to think about.

But being around Jeremy makes me feel…

With a shiver, Alison pulled the covers back up to her chin.

"Alive again," she whispered into the silence.

What do I do? I want to feel alive. But this is too soon. And it could end with me feeling sad all over again when Jeremy leaves and I'm left alone. And, Father, you know that I've had enough sadness for a lifetime. I've cried more tears than I could ever count.

Alison rubbed her feet together, now feeling cold all over. Like the empty chair next to her at Mark Harmen's office, the vacant space where Connor used to sleep caused her heart to hurt.

I still miss Connor every day. Every single day.

I can't be ready to move on if I still feel this way, if I still miss him this much. Can I?

Wednesday morning, after Alison dropped Nicholas off at school and returned home, she was surprised to hear

Jeremy walking around upstairs. The other mornings he'd been out at the river by that time. She cleaned up the breakfast dishes and eventually heard his footsteps coming down the stairs.

She glanced up as he walked through the kitchen, pursing her lips to keep from grinning at the sight of him decked out in his waders, fishing hat and green flannel shirt. Only his muddy boots were missing from the ensemble. He hadn't shaved since the day before, so more than a five-o'clock shadow covered his handsome face.

"What?" he said.

"Nothing. You just definitely look like a mountain man today," Alison teased. Jeremy looked down at his apparel and then stroked his chin.

"I suppose you're right. Can this mountain man get a cup of coffee to go?"

Alison nodded and sifted through the cabinets for a portable coffee cup. "Thanks so much for fishing with Nic yesterday. He loved it."

"I did, too. He's such a great kid, Alison. I like spending time with him."

She nodded. "The same goes for him. So it looks like you're getting a later start today, huh?"

"Yeah. I was a little tired this morning. When would you like to work on our chili?"

"If you give me the list of ingredients we need, I'll pick them up in town today. Then maybe we could do a test run this weekend. My parents sometimes come over for dinner—"

"So they could be our guinea pigs when it comes to experimenting with our chili recipe?" Jeremy said with a laugh and Alison laughed with him.

"I'm sure they'd be willing. I could ask them to come Saturday. What do you think?"

"That sounds good to me. I'd love to meet them anyway."

"Would you?" Alison asked.

"Sure. I've heard a lot about them from you and Nicholas. And they're probably curious about your guest, right?"

Alison felt her cheeks turn red. "Well…they worry about me and Nicholas, you know. So, yes, I'm sure meeting you would give them some peace of mind."

"Then by all means, invite them. I'll see if I can win them over with my cooking."

Jeremy caught her gaze and held it, sending shivers down Alison's spine.

"What's on your agenda today?" Jeremy wondered.

"I'm going over to the church in a little while. During the fall months, we do a soup kitchen on Wednesdays and Fridays. I'm scheduled to help serve this afternoon."

Jeremy looked down at his waders. "I wish I'd have known. I'd love to help out, but I'm dressed for the river."

Alison shook her head. "We've got it covered. The fish are waiting for you," she said.

"Maybe I could go with you next week since I'll still be here," Jeremy offered.

Alison could imagine the wagging tongues if she showed up to serve with Jeremy. But the thought didn't deter her from saying yes.

"That would be nice, Jeremy. If you want to."

Alison filled the coffee container and held it out for Jeremy. Their hands brushed as he took it from her, and one glance at Jeremy told Alison he'd felt it just like she had. She immediately turned her attention to the sink.

"Thank you, Alison," Jeremy said, his voice just a tad unsteady. Alison couldn't speak, knowing her own voice would be just as unsteady, if not more so. The hairs on her neck stood straight just from his close proximity.

She wished he'd go ahead and make his way down to the river.

Or kiss her. One of the two.

Chapter 9

Alison wiped down the tables in the church lunchroom where she and the team had just served about one hundred and fifty hungry people.

"Well, that was a great turnout," Mary Margaret said as she swept.

"Absolutely," Michelle agreed, setting chairs upside down on the tables to make it easier for Mary Margaret. "We had just enough food. I think we'll need to plan to have a little more next time, though. I'd rather have too much than not enough."

"I think you're right," Alison said as she tossed the dishrag into the to-be-washed pile. "Once word gets out that our soup kitchen is back open for the fall, we'll have even more people. Even if attendance ebbs and flows, I think we're going to consistently have close to a hundred people. We need more volunteers for serving and more contributions to the food pantry."

"There were so many families!" Mary Margaret said with dismay. "It breaks my heart to see those children."

"I know what you mean," Michelle said gently. "But remember, it warms the Father's heart to see those children—and their parents—being fed. I'm so thankful our church wants to meet the needs of those who are struggling in our community. I'll talk to Kirsten in the administration office about putting something in the bulletin next week regarding needing more donations on a regular basis. If we can get some help gathering ingredients, I know plenty of people in the church would be happy to help cook and put some simple meals together."

"What's on the menu for Friday night?" Alison asked.

"Spaghetti and meatballs. Actually, the youth group will be helping prepare and serve," Michelle told them. Mary Margaret loaded the dishtowels in a basket and carried them off to her car; she'd offered to wash them at home. Alison and Michelle dragged the mop bucket to the middle of the room and decided to split the job in half. Alison dunked her mop in the soapy water and started sliding it across the left side of the floor.

"I might as well tell you, Jeremy's staying an extra week and entering the chili cook-off with me."

"Wow! So he was up for it, huh?"

"Yeah. I told him he didn't have to stay for the festival— I just needed some help preparing—but he insisted. He said it sounds fun to him. Nic is thrilled."

"It will be fun. Are you excited about it?" Michelle asked.

"Oh sure. But I'm a little afraid we won't win after he's done all this for me. He's paying to stay next week and everything. Even though I wish he didn't have to."

"You're providing breakfast and lodging for him, Ali. And sometimes dinner! And besides, you need the funds," Michelle pointed out. Alison sighed and plunged the mop in the water again.

"I know. I'm not really in a position to say no to payment. Still, even if we don't win, I hope the week is a positive experience. I don't see how it's been very relaxing for him. Yesterday he repaired the loose step on the back deck, and last night he changed the front porch light for me when we realized it had burned out. He keeps helping me, doing things with Nicholas, eating dinner with us—not exactly a quiet week in the mountains."

"He doesn't have to do any of those things if he doesn't

want to, Alison. He's *choosing* to do them. That says something about the man's character. And he's the one deciding to stay for the festival. And the festival is always a great time! He'll love it!"

"We're going to do a practice run on our chili, and Mom and Dad are coming to be our taste testers Saturday night."

Michelle whistled. "That ought to be interesting!"

"I hope Dad isn't too hard on him."

"Your parents love you and have been a wonderful support system for you and Nicholas. And besides that, I have a feeling this chef of yours can hold his own. Give your dad a little latitude, Ali. He's looking out for you."

Alison bit back the retort that she was a grown woman and a mother. She knew her parents had been there for her every step of the way.

"He's not *my* chef, Michelle," Alison said with a sigh that had just a twinge of longing. "But you're right—I need to be patient with Mom and Dad. They've helped me so much."

"Boundaries and grace," Michelle said once the only sound in the room was that of the mops sloshing on the floor. "It's a tricky balance. It's okay to set boundaries, but you can't forget to extend grace."

On the way home after picking up Nicholas from school, Alison still mulled over Michelle's words.

Boundaries and grace. That is *a tricky balance.*

She pulled into the driveway and Nic nearly jumped from the car.

"Can I fish with Jeremy today, Mom?"

Alison caught up with him on the porch. "I don't know, Nic. He may be out on the river somewhere. If he comes back to the house, and *only if he asks you*, you can go down to the river. For now, I want you to tackle that homework."

With a groan, Nic dragged his backpack into the house and made his way to the table, where Alison set out some apple slices for him to snack on while he worked on his homework. Jeremy was nowhere to be found, so Alison supposed he was still out fishing. She hesitated as she inspected the contents of the refrigerator, unsure whether to just assume Jeremy would be joining them for dinner. As time ticked by and Jeremy didn't return, she decided to keep dinner light. She made some chicken noodle soup and threw together some grilled cheese and tomato sandwiches. Jeremy walked in after she and Nic were already eating.

"We have plenty if you want to eat, Jeremy," Alison immediately offered. His face was pink from the sun and he looked worn out. He shook his head.

"Thanks, Alison, but I'm going to head upstairs for a shower. I may come down and make a sandwich later. The fish were jumping today and the weather was perfect, though I think I got more sun than I planned on. I went for a hike mid-afternoon and saw an incredibly beautiful waterfall!"

"You must have gone all the way to Pebble Creek Falls! That's quite a hike," Alison said, enjoying Jeremy's flushed, rustic look. She had to admit that there wasn't much *not* to like about the ruggedly handsome man standing in her kitchen.

"Could I fish with you tomorrow after school, Jeremy?" Nic asked, conveniently ignoring the consternation on Alison's face at his inability to wait for Jeremy to ask him.

"If it's okay with your mom. I'll make sure I'm back at the house by four o'clock."

Both Nic and Jeremy turned to look at Alison, Nic's face pleading with her to say yes. She gave up.

"If you guys stay where I can see you while I'm cooking dinner, then sure."

"Yes!" Nic clapped his hands. With a nod to Alison, Jeremy excused himself to go upstairs. Because he'd finished his homework, Alison allowed Nic to go to the basement and play video games for just a short while before bedtime. She loaded the dishwasher and wiped down the counters before pulling on a fleece jacket and stepping on the back porch for a moment alone. The moon shone down on the river, the water gurgled and the fallen leaves rustled in the breeze.

She wondered about Jeremy upstairs. She'd missed having him at the dinner table. But that was ridiculous, she scolded herself.

He barely knows me. I barely know him. He is not a replacement for Connor. It's just...I guess I like having him around.

The glass door behind her slid open and Alison swirled around.

There stood the very person she couldn't seem to stop thinking about.

"Jeremy, um, did you come down for a sandwich?" she asked, unable to think of anything else to say.

He stepped out on the porch and closed the door behind him.

"I did. Is it okay if I join you out here for a minute?"

She looked past him at the empty kitchen and thought of Nic in the basement.

"Sure. I mean, of course you can." Her words came out fast and high-pitched and she didn't even recognize her own voice.

Calm down, girl! The fact that you're alone in the moonlight with this sort-of-amazing chef means nothing. Just two people hanging out on the back porch.

Nothing out of the ordinary.

What am I saying? Of course this is out of the ordinary!

She kept her gaze out on the water and nowhere near Jeremy.

"Do you miss Connor?"

The question nearly knocked her over.

Alison still didn't look in Jeremy's direction. "All the time," she answered honestly.

They were both quiet for a moment. But his direct question stirred some bravery in Alison. If he could be so direct, so could she.

"Have you ever been married? Or come close?" she asked, peeking over at Jeremy next to her.

He leaned against the wood post and crossed his arms. "No, I've never been married. And I haven't really come close. I did have a rather long-term, serious relationship in my early twenties, but it didn't work out."

"Is marriage not something that interests you?"

He looked down. "I've always assumed I'd get married someday. And have a family. But work has been my focus for many years now."

Alison didn't say anything.

"Nic wonders if you might ever get married again," Jeremy said in a low voice. Alison turned to face him.

"He said that to you?" she said in disbelief.

He nodded. "Does that bother you?" he asked. "He might need someone to talk to, and I enjoy talking with him. But only if you're okay with it."

Alison inhaled. *He's right. Nic needs to be able to share his feelings.*

She desperately wanted to ask whether Nic seemed upset by the idea of her remarrying and what Jeremy had said in response. But the moment didn't feel right to push for more.

"If Nic chooses to confide in you, then I'm not going to say he can't as long as you would tell me if there's anything I should be worried about. With Nic, I mean."

"I would tell you," Jeremy said, his tone solemn. A breeze blew past Alison and she shivered.

"I love the changing of the leaf colors. I love the fall season, but I always miss the warmth of summer. Summer never seems long enough to me," she said. Jeremy suddenly stepped off the porch. He turned to face her and held out his hand.

"Do you want to walk down to the water? It's so beautiful out here at night." His gaze met hers and he waited.

Alison felt like a teenager, nervous, staring out at his open hand and wondering what it would feel like to place hers in it.

She looked at him, and despite the arguments in her head, she felt drawn to him. She reached out and placed her hand in his.

"Mom!" the door slid open. "What are you guys *doing* out here? My game is over. Can I play another one?"

Alison instantly dropped Jeremy's hand, knowing her face was probably beet red. Good thing it was dark. She stepped back toward the door. "What? Oh, um, no, Nic. It's bedtime."

"Aww, Mom! One more?"

She pushed Nic back inside without looking at Jeremy.

Jeremy didn't move from where he stood below the deck. He just stared into the warm house until he saw Alison and Nic disappear around the corner toward the basement. He shook his head.

What was I doing? Trying to hold her hand? I might as well be a lovesick teenager. This is getting ludicrous.

Jeremy turned and stomped down to the river. The moonlight lit the path and he didn't stop until he reached the water's edge.

He reprimanded himself soundly, but his argument couldn't drown out the picture in his mind of Alison reaching out and placing her hand in his.

She did that on her own. If Nic hadn't opened the door, she probably would have walked down to the water with me.

And I would have kissed her.

Jeremy knew that without a doubt.

This was getting too intense. And he knew he wasn't hiding his feelings. She could tell he liked her. But he knew nothing could come of it. *For her sake and mine—and Nic's—I need to try harder to control my feelings.*

Jeremy reached down, picked up a stone and threw it as far down the river as he could. He had to wonder…if Alison knew all the thoughts rushing through his mind, would she want him to hold back? Or would she have wanted that kiss as much as he did?

He couldn't know the answer to that question, as much as he wished he could.

Maybe he was finally feeling ready for a family of his own, finally seeing that he wanted more out of life. *I came up here because I was feeling worn out and needed a break. I wasn't looking for a girlfriend for goodness' sake.... And even if I did try to pursue Alison, she said that she still misses Connor all the time. She's not ready.* Jeremy's thoughts turned upward, into prayer.

Lord, I don't want to hurt Alison. And I don't want to be disappointed. So if you could cool this attraction I have for her, that would be really helpful.

Chapter 10

Saturday morning, Alison yawned as she padded upstairs from the basement to the kitchen. Nic had begged
for French toast the night before. She pulled out a carton of
eggs from the fridge and smiled as she cracked them and
turned on her skillet. The past two days had been, in her
opinion, excellent in every way. Thursday Nic and Jeremy
had fished together after school and come in for a dinner of
pasta primavera, joking and laughing all through the meal.
Friday night had been even more fun. Jeremy had helped
them make homemade pizza, then they all had played board
games before turning on a movie. Nic had fallen asleep
halfway through, and Alison had roused him, forcing him
to go on downstairs to bed. Then she and Jeremy had finished watching the movie together.

Now she paused, trying to suppress the flutters in her
stomach as she remembered last night.

While watching the movie, she'd positioned herself
firmly in the comfy chair to avoid any temptation to sit
next to Jeremy and let her emotions get the best of her. And
to Jeremy's credit, he'd stayed rooted on the sofa across
from her.

But still.

Every minute alone had felt charged with electricity.
Every stolen glance at Jeremy, every time she caught him
stealing a glance at her—she'd forgotten how it felt, those
first few delicious moments of attraction.

"Mom, I'm tired," Nic said in a monotone as he walked barefoot into the kitchen, his hair a mess. He pulled open the refrigerator and reached for the jug of orange juice.

"Good morning," Alison said cheerfully, smoothing back Nicholas's ruffled hair. He looked up at her dubiously.

"You're happy," he said after a moment. Alison chuckled self-consciously.

"Of course I am. You're here."

Once he had a glass of juice, she put her hands on his shoulders and directed the lethargic eight-year-old to the living room.

"Why don't you watch cartoons or something? I'm going to fry some bacon to go with our French toast."

"Has Jeremy been downstairs yet?" Nic asked. Alison shook her head.

"Nope, so I'd better start breakfast. This is a bed-and-breakfast after all," she said with a teasing grin. Nic smiled back at her.

Alison turned her attention back to the task at hand. Soon the kitchen smelled of bacon, maple syrup and cinnamon. She hummed while she worked, looking forward to the afternoon she and Jeremy had planned for preparing chili. Not even the daunting thought of her parents meeting Jeremy could dampen her spirits.

"What's our schedule today?"

Alison looked up from where she worked at the stove, and her heart skipped a beat at hearing Jeremy's voice.

She remembered the food and quickly flipped a piece of French toast.

"Well, we have everything to make our first test batch," she said over her shoulder. "My parents will probably come over rather early. Maybe two or three o'clock. I told them we'd aim to have dinner around four. They won't want to stay too late so an early dinner will be best. I was thinking we'd also make a batch of cornbread to go with the chili."

"Sounds delicious. And what will we serve for dessert?"

Alison didn't answer for a moment. The fact that *they* were serving together made her feel both excited and, in all honesty, a little guilt-ridden.

This had been her and Connor's kitchen. They'd cooked side by side for many guests. Now here stood someone else. Someone she liked. Someone she wanted to spend time with. Someone she wanted to cook with.

Alison licked her lips. "My mother's bringing dessert. She insisted. But you're in luck because she's making her famous lemon bars. Trust me, you want to try them."

Jeremy smiled and snagged a slice of bacon from the dish. "Can't wait."

Alison swatted at his hand. "Go watch TV with Nic. Breakfast is almost ready."

After breakfast, Alison shooed Nicholas outside to play while she and Jeremy got to work in the kitchen. As Nicholas dribbled a basketball on the back porch, both she and Jeremy donned aprons and studied Jeremy's recipe, with his friend Ethan's suggestions.

"So many spices!" Alison noted. Jeremy nodded without speaking, his mind obviously on the recipe.

Alison had a feeling that Jeremy was going to approach this challenge intensely. She didn't mind.

"Are you sure Ethan recommended using cocoa?" she said with doubt in her voice. Jeremy glanced up at her with a smile.

"You're going to have to trust me on this one, Ali."

Alison's mouth went dry.

He'd called her *Ali*. Something Connor had always called her. Something close friends and family called her. Yet, it sounded right coming from Jeremy. At this point, even if she'd only known him for a few days, she couldn't deny that he at least felt like a real friend to her.

Alison coughed and left Jeremy poring over the recipe while she drank a glass of water. Once she felt a bit more composed, she tapped her fingers on the counter.

"Okay, Chef. Where do you want me?"

Jeremy clasped his hands and looked over the organized ingredients lining the countertop. "All right. You're at the chopping station. First I need you to chop a couple of onions and mince three cloves of garlic. I'll start by browning the meat. We'll go from there."

Alison opened the back door so she could easily hear Nicholas in the backyard, popped out her head to remind him to stay where she could see him and then grabbed a knife and an onion.

For the most part, she and Jeremy worked in comfortable silence. Alison had tried to keep up a steady stream of chitchat, but she soon realized how focused Jeremy was in the kitchen. Talking too much seemed to distract him. He was on a mission to create the best chili in Estes Park.

Once all the meat was browned and cooked with the onions, garlic, green chiles and just a hint of jalapeño, they put the mixture in a large stockpot and added a host of other ingredients and spices. When the chili came to a boil, Jeremy lowered the heat to simmer. Alison tidied their workspace so they could begin to make the cornbread.

More than once, Nicholas came crashing through the door, starving for snacks and wanting to see how things were coming along. Once the chili was simmering and the pan of cornbread was baking in the oven, Jeremy joined Nic outside, where they gathered some wood to light the fire pit that evening. Alison told the guys that they could roast marshmallows at sunset.

They were still outside when Alison heard a knock and then the front door open. Her parents were right on time.

"I'm in the kitchen!" she called out, stirring the chili.

"Something smells delicious!" her mother announced as she walked into the room. Alison smiled. Her mother, Jolene Clark, was a small woman, shorter than her by several inches. Small but wiry. Her mother had spunk, something Alison wished she'd inherited more of. Her mom dropped her purse on the counter and shook back her short, nutmeg-colored hair that had most certainly been treated by a box of Lady Clairol recently. The color suited her mother. Alison wiped her hands on her apron and moved to kiss her cheek.

"Let's hope it's the best chili you've ever tasted," Alison quipped. Her father gave her a hug, then quickly walked to the back door, no doubt wondering about Nicholas and Jeremy.

"They're right by the river, Dad," Alison assured him. "They're gathering some wood for the fire pit. Nic wants to roast marshmallows later."

"I see them. I think I'll go out and introduce myself," her father said, opening the door and stepping out onto the deck.

"Dad—" Alison began. Her mother held up her hand.

"Let him go, Ali. He might as well go meet the fisherman. He's been curious about him for days."

Alison sighed in resignation.

"You can call him Jeremy, Mom, rather than 'the fisherman.' He's really nice. I hope you like him."

Alison's mother's eyebrows instantly raised. "Why? Do you like him?"

Alison flushed. "Of course. I just said he's nice."

Concern etched her mother's face. "I'm sure he is. But, Alison, do you really think—"

"Mom," Alison said in a patient voice. "Could we hold off on the questions till after you've met him?"

Her mom looked surprised by Alison's comment, but she gradually nodded. "That sounds fair. As long as you know that questions *will* be coming."

Alison walked to the glass door and looked out at her father and Jeremy in the distance. "I never doubted that for a second."

She watched the two of them talking, wondering what they were saying, wondering if it was about her.

Stop worrying! Jeremy's a capable, amiable man. He's perfectly able to converse with Dad. I need to stop fretting over this meeting and doubting myself every second.

Alison turned around. "Mom, do you want to help me set the table?"

Her mother jumped up to help. The spicy smell of chili filled the kitchen, and Alison breathed in the scent. With a cool nip in the air, the windows open, chili simmering on the stove and cornbread turning golden in the oven, Alison felt that autumn had descended on the Mountain View B&B, and to her, the season seemed full of possibility. She hummed as she stirred the chili, and her mother moved to the dining room, putting together simple place settings.

Alison had just set a basket of cornbread squares on the table when the back door slid open and in came her dad followed by Nicholas and Jeremy.

"Mom! Grandpa wants to learn to fly-fish! He's going to come over next week and go fishing with Jeremy!" Nicholas exclaimed.

"Really?" Alison said with a quizzical look in her dad's direction. He shrugged.

"Well, you know I enjoy fishing. Jeremy explained the ins and outs of fly-fishing and I think I would like it. The exercise would be good for me."

"Oh, yes," Alison's mother said, her head bobbing. "We like to stay as active as possible." Her mother reached out her hand to Jeremy. "Jeremy, I'm so pleased to meet you. Please, call me Jolene."

"And I insist you call me Eli," her father broke in. "No more of this 'Mr. Clark,' Jeremy."

Jeremy grinned at both of them. "Eli and Jolene, then."

Alison looked at the three adults standing in front of her, more than a little shocked by her parents' warmth toward Jeremy.

I can't believe Jeremy won Dad over so quickly! Then

again, why should she be surprised? He'd won her over, hadn't he?

Jeremy checked the chili. Nicholas sat waiting at the dining room table with his grandparents. Alison stood nervously, watching Jeremy raise a spoon to his lips to taste the chili.

"Well?" she demanded. He lowered the spoon.

"Hmm," he answered.

"Hmm?" Alison echoed, her curiosity rising. "What does that mean? Is it any good?"

Jeremy's face was void of emotion. "You tell me."

Alison grabbed a clean spoon, dunked it into the chili pot, then blew on it to cool the steaming mouthful.

Jeremy crossed his arms and waited.

Alison relished the bite. A perfect blend of spice and heat inundated her senses.

"What do you think?" Jeremy asked, smiling as though he knew her answer.

"I think we've got a culinary success on our hands," Alison said, trying to sound professional. She and Jeremy looked at each other and then burst out laughing.

"It's fantastic!" Alison exclaimed.

"That's the best chili I've ever tasted," Jeremy said, his countenance elated.

"Come on," Alison said, composing herself. "Let's serve and give everyone a chance to taste this award-winning dish."

"We haven't won any awards yet, Ali," Jeremy said.

"Jeremy, this chili is scrumptious. Even if we don't win a blue ribbon, I'm thrilled with how it turned out." Alison suddenly realized how close Jeremy was standing to her. Her heart pounded like a war drum.

"We make a good team," Jeremy said in a relaxed voice. Alison could hardly breathe. Her parents and her son were right around the corner. She could hear Nicholas's prattle from where she stood in the kitchen. The combined heat of the stove and Jeremy's presence overwhelmed her.

"What if I told you I wanted to kiss you right now, Alison?" Jeremy leaned closer and whispered. Alison tried to swallow but wasn't quite able to.

Alison looked downward. "Jeremy," she kept her tone equally low to avoid anyone else in the house hearing her. "I wouldn't want to give—"

"Ali, do you need any help?" her mother called out from the dining room. Alison shook her head, then realized she needed to actually speak.

"Um, no, Mom. We're bringing out the food now," she said loudly. She concentrated on ladling a generous helping of chili into a bowl, then handed it to Jeremy to place on the tray she'd set on the counter. Once the tray was filled, Alison watched Jeremy carry it to the dining room. She stared at his back, only aware at that moment that her hands were trembling.

Father, please give me the strength I need at this moment. I wanted Jeremy to kiss me, and I'm just not sure if I'm right or wrong to feel that way. I don't know what to do. How are we going to stay under the same roof for another week without one of us saying something about how we're really feeling?

Alison heard Jeremy's voice carry from the dining room.

Another week? Good grief—how am I supposed to last the evening?

Chapter 11

Jeremy placed some dirty dishes in the sink and checked to make sure the coffee was brewing. Jolene walked in with the last of the chili bowls and set them aside.

"The coffee smells delicious. My daughter does love her coffee," she commented. Jeremy nodded. Jolene took the foil off the pan of lemon bars she'd brought.

"Hand me a stack of those dessert plates from the cupboard to the right, please, Jeremy. I'll serve dessert."

Jeremy found the plates. "What else can I do to help?" he asked. Jolene nodded toward the coffeemaker.

"Set the cream and sugar on Ali's tray, along with spoons, and you can carry that out to the den once the coffee's ready."

They worked in silence for a moment, with Jolene putting the thick, tart bars on each plate.

"You seem at home here," she said. Jeremy wondered how to respond. Her words had held no accusation, but he felt unsure.

"I've enjoyed the week. I'm really going to miss Alison and Nicholas once I head back to Denver," Jeremy stated honestly.

"They're going to miss you," Jolene said, her tone light but even.

"I'm looking forward to the festival," Jeremy said, his throat dry. "It should be a lot of fun. And I think Alison and I have a shot at winning the chili cook-off."

Jolene smiled at him, but she didn't seem completely open. Jeremy could sense some strain. "Oh, you have more than a shot if those judges have any sense. That chili you two created was absolutely delicious. And I appreciate your going to the trouble of helping Alison compete."

"It's my pleasure. As I said, I'm enjoying my time here."

"Yes," Jolene said slowly. The silence between them felt heavy, and Jeremy couldn't shake off his anxiety as he waited for Jolene's next words. "Jeremy, my daughter has suffered much in the past few years. She's experienced more grief than I can even imagine. So has Nicholas. I would hate for the two of them to get overly attached to you—only for you to leave and for both of them to endure more sadness."

Jeremy wouldn't let himself bristle at the words. He'd said them to himself over and over, hadn't he? While he understood and respected Jolene for speaking up on her daughter's behalf, that didn't lessen the disappointment he felt at the thought of pulling away from Alison when every impulse he had was the opposite.

"Have you ever been married?" Jolene asked.

Jeremy guessed an interrogation was coming. He shook his head.

"No, I haven't. I haven't even come close. But I would like to be married and have a family one day."

"I see," Jolene said. She poured four cups of coffee, and Jeremy set them on the tray. "Are you a believer, Jeremy?"

He nodded. "My faith is very important to me. I know faith is important to Alison too."

"To Eli and me, too," Jolene told him. "It was Alison's faith that kept her going when she was holding on by just a fragile emotional thread after Connor passed. The fact that she's determined to run this place and that she's doing such a great job raising Nicholas—well, I'm proud of my daughter. But we all have our limits."

Jeremy had a feeling that it went without saying that another heartbreak would be past Alison's limit. He wished he could convey to Jolene that that would never happen with him.

But he couldn't.

Not when his return trip home was non-negotiable.

"Denver's not that far, you know," Jeremy mustered the courage to say the words he was thinking. Jolene cocked her head to the side and studied him.

"No, it's not. That's true."

"I like Alison, Jolene. I would never want to hurt her."

Jolene nodded. "I believe you. But she's been hurt enough…even unintentionally. Keep that in mind. And you have to be extra cautious when a child's feelings are involved. And from what I see with you and Nicholas, his feelings are involved."

Guilt swept over Jeremy. There was no denying Nicholas's tendency to eagerly follow him around. And Jeremy enjoyed his company. For the first time maybe ever, Jeremy had started thinking about how nice it would be to have a son of his own. Someone to fish with, someone to show him how to do the things his father had shown him how to do. And Nicholas seemed to need a friend.

Maybe Jeremy did, too.

"I'll take the tray into the den," Jolene said quietly. He hadn't even noticed her reach for the tray. He stood alone with his thoughts in the kitchen. After a moment, he heard Jolene call out Nicholas's name and then descend into the basement. Jeremy placed both palms on the kitchen counter.

What am I going to do?

With a gruff sigh, he picked up a stack of napkins and headed for the den. He stopped in the hallway at the sound of Alison's frustrated voice.

"Dad, I have a feeling things are about to turn around."

"You just told me that the banker advised you to sell!" he said in a strained whisper.

"He said *to think about it* if…if things don't pick up.

He said to give myself a timeline. And I plan to. I know I'm losing money. But you don't understand…this place… I can't give it up."

"It's just a house, Ali. I know it feels like more than that to you—but it's walls and rooms and they're draining your bank account. What matters is taking care of Nic."

"I *am* taking care of Nic."

Jeremy winced at the bite in Alison's tone.

"I know you are. I just don't want to see you lose everything because of an emotional connection to this place. You could move in with your mother and me—"

"We've talked about this, Dad. I'm beyond grateful for the help you two provide, but if at all possible, I want a home just for me and Nicholas. Maybe that's unrealistic in the long term, I don't know. But I'm not ready to let go of Connor yet!" Her voice choked and Jeremy froze, unable to breathe during the silence that followed.

"Honey." Eli's voice had softened, but his words came out firm and strong. "We're talking about the house, not Connor."

"I know." Alison's voice was hollow.

"This is your decision to make. We can talk about it more later."

Jeremy knew it was time he made his entrance, if only to help ease the tension. He strolled into the den.

"I brought some napkins," he said, holding them up. Alison nodded, although the clouds didn't scatter from her eyes. "Those lemon bars look delicious," Jeremy continued.

"Lemon bars! Yum!" Nicholas exclaimed as he and Jolene joined them. Nicholas's enthusiasm filled the room as he chomped on dessert and bounced between talking with Jeremy to talking with his grandparents. Alison sat silently next to Jeremy on the sofa.

Lord, how can I help her at this moment?

"Alison," Jeremy said. She turned to face him. Her blond hair fell over her shoulders, and she was sitting close enough that Jeremy could see the sprinkling of freckles on her cheeks. Jeremy tried to give a word for how she looked in that moment.

Fragile came to mind. Along with *beautiful*.

Focus, Jeremy.

"Would it be okay if I join you and Nic for church tomorrow? I'd like to see this church of yours."

Her smile sent a flutter through Jeremy. But as he reached for a mug of coffee, he realized Eli and Jolene were both staring at him. And neither of them were smiling.

Jeremy only hoped they'd be filled with Christian generosity of spirit when they saw him walk through the church doors with their daughter the next morning.

After insisting on bedtime for Nicholas after his third cup of water, Alison wearily climbed the stairs to the first floor of the house, knowing the sink full of dishes needed her attention. Her shoulders ached from the stress she felt over her conversation with her dad, along with the hours spent under the prying eyes of her parents, who scrutinized her every movement when Jeremy was in the room.

What was I expecting? They're curious about Jeremy. They're worried about me.

So am I.

She turned the corner and stopped short. Jeremy stood at the sink, in up to his elbows in dirty dishes. He smiled at her.

"Hey, I thought I'd clean up."

She bit her lip.

Why do I feel like crying, God? I'm so unsteady. Please give me strength.

"Thanks, Jeremy," she said, grabbing a washcloth and wiping down the counters. They worked in silence, listening to the sound of the wind increasing outside.

"The temperature is supposed to drop tonight," Jeremy

said as he finished the dishes and dried his hands. Alison walked to the door and looked out at the dark sky.

"Will that affect your fishing?" she wondered. Jeremy pulled out a chair at the breakfast table and sat down.

"Not really. I can dress for the weather. Now if it starts to sleet or snow, that may change things. But as for tomorrow, I have other plans."

"Oh?" Alison turned around, curious. Jeremy smiled and pointed to the chair across from him.

"Will you sit with me, Alison?"

Alison wished she didn't feel so nervous. Nervous to be with Jeremy. But she'd rather face the nerves than go downstairs alone. So she sat down.

"What are these plans you have for tomorrow?"

"Well, you've said I can go to church with you and Nicholas. And you've cooked for me all week. Breakfast, lunch and dinner—which was more than you bargained for. If you'll let me, I'd like to cook dinner for you and Nic."

Alison tapped her lips playfully. "You have to know… my expectations are pretty high. I know that Romano's is a four-star restaurant."

Jeremy laughed. "I'll take that challenge. So, dinner tomorrow, all right? Any requests?"

Alison looked Jeremy over for a moment. He seemed so relaxed at her table, in her kitchen. The green in his shirt brought out the green hues in his eyes. He'd rolled up the sleeves to wash dishes. And a faint scent of cologne drifted from him.

Why do you have to be so adorable?

"Surprise me."

"Can I ask you something, Alison?"

She felt too warm and cozy at that moment to refuse, so she just nodded.

"Why a B&B? What made you and Connor decide to run this kind of business?"

For once, Alison didn't feel a twinge at the mention of

Connor. "You know, it's just something we'd always talked about. How fun it would be, how we'd meet so many interesting people, how we'd be working side by side. I think that was what appealed to me the most. We had all these grand plans. Connor wanted to take a cooking course so we could expand our breakfast menu. But…that never happened," her voice faltered. She stood, moved to the refrigerator, pulled out the carton of milk and poured herself a glass.

"What about you? Have you ever thought of owning your own restaurant?"

Jeremy shrugged. "I can't say I haven't thought about it. Probably every chef does at one point or another. But I've seen how much pressure the administrative side of that can be for Leo—Leo Romano, that is. I enjoy cooking more than doing the administration part. I thought about teaching for a while, actually. I like helping others learn to cook. But in the end, I stayed at Romano's. I love running a thriving kitchen."

Alison leaned against the counter. "I love running this B&B. I just hope it works out."

Alison didn't miss the slightly uncomfortable look that crossed Jeremy's face. "Alison, I have something of a confession to make. I…well, I overheard a little of your conversation with your dad today."

Alison was too tired to feel upset. And the weight of financial difficulty looming over her had taken such a toll that, at this point, she didn't care if Jeremy knew.

"Well, I'm not ready to throw in the towel yet," she answered, struggling to keep her tone positive.

"Good. I wouldn't want you to," Jeremy responded.

Alison blinked. "Really? Why do you say that?"

"It's a great place. Great location. And you're a wonderful hostess."

"Thanks, Jeremy." Alison was warmed by his praise. "You're not a bad houseguest, you know."

Jeremy chuckled and stood, pushing his chair back under the table. "You mean you don't mind that I've invaded your family dinners and movie nights?" Alison couldn't even join in laughing with him. Jeremy's smile caused tingles to crawl up her neck.

"Not to mention the fact that you've fixed things around the house," Alison began, "taught my son to fly-fish, been gracious enough to stay longer to enter a chili cook-off and I just caught you washing dishes—I don't mind, Jeremy."

His chuckle faded, and Jeremy moved in front of her.

"Having you here has been…" Alison froze and couldn't finish her thought.

"I keep telling myself not to like you so much," he said quietly. "It's not working."

A rollercoaster of emotions plummeted inside of Alison.

"I feel the same way," she admitted. She tried to concentrate on breathing but Jeremy's close proximity made that impossible.

"Can I kiss you, Alison?" he asked, his voice just above a whisper as he leaned down toward her. Alison closed her eyes.

"Yes," she whispered.

Chapter 12

Alison entered the church sanctuary, feeling like an exhibit at the zoo. She wasn't sure if it was just her imagination, but she felt like every eye in the building was glued on her—and Jeremy and Nicholas—as they filed into a pew on the fourth row, right next to her parents. They smiled politely at Jeremy, but Alison saw them exchange one of those glances. The kind where her parents basically had an entire conversation with just a look between them.

They were running a little late, but Alison didn't care. She figured that might stave off the unstoppable curiosity of the church people who knew her so well.

The pianist had just begun to play and folks were finding their seats. Michelle rushed over and sat on the other side of Alison, leaning across her to speak to Jeremy.

"Hi there!" Michelle said brightly. Jeremy shook her hand.

"Jeremy Mitchell," he said. "Nice to meet you."

"Michelle Evans. I've heard so much about you!"

Alison poked her.

"I mean, I've heard a couple things. Nothing major," Michelle backtracked. Jeremy raised an eyebrow.

"All good things," she continued. "Will you guys be staying for the potluck after services?"

Alison looked sideways at Jeremy. "I forgot to tell you there was a potluck today. Actually, I forgot about the potluck. I don't know, Michelle. I didn't bring anything."

Michelle nudged her. "No one cares about that, Ali, and you know it. Besides your mom probably brought enough to feed all of us. Didn't you, Jolene?" Michelle whispered down the pew.

"There's plenty," Jolene agreed curtly.

"Well, I'd like to stay," Jeremy inserted.

"Mom! If Shawn's staying, I want to stay!" Nicholas whined.

Oh please, everyone!

Alison nodded. "Sure. Sounds fun."

Michelle sat back when the worship leader stood. The congregation followed in suit, and Alison let herself be swept away by the music. She loved hearing the rise of so many voices in their small church. The building was old, though it had been refurbished. Still, the voices carried all through the church during the worship portion.

She forced herself to stay focused on the music and the message, rather than the man next to her—though it was a challenge. As soon as the service ended, a steady stream of churchgoers made their way to greet Jeremy. Although Alison felt certain that inquisitiveness drove some of the attenders, she also knew the people of River Community went out of their way to make all visitors feel welcome, and she was thankful to see firsthand that same response for Jeremy.

As they walked side by side to the church dining hall, he told her, "This is possibly the friendliest church I've ever been to."

Alison smiled. "I know. We're a welcoming bunch, what can I say?"

Mary Margaret immediately planted her family across from them at one of the tables, and Michelle stationed herself and Shawn next to them. Alison mechanically ate her fried chicken and coleslaw, all the while worrying that Jeremy would be annoyed by the bombardment of questions coming from every direction, but he seemed to enjoy the conversation.

"The boys are wondering if Nic can come over and play this afternoon," Michelle said to Alison while Mary Margaret extracted a detailed history of Jeremy's life.

"Well, Jeremy's making dinner for us tonight," Alison said, as she tried to catch what Jeremy was saying to Mary Margaret.

"Oh?"

Alison turned at the heightened interest in Michelle's tone. She lowered her voice to keep their words private.

"Yeah. He said he'd like to."

"I see," Michelle said after a moment.

"Do you think I'm making a mistake?" Alison whispered.

Michelle looked at her with something that resembled sympathy. "It's only dinner, Ali."

"I know." Alison sighed. "Still, I feel like I'm getting more invested every day."

"Do you really like him?" Michelle's words were barely above a whisper.

Guilt rushed over Alison as she remembered the kiss she and Jeremy had shared the night before. Did she like Jeremy?

To the point of distraction. I can't stop thinking about the guy.

She held back that thought and listened to Jeremy next to her, talking about fly-fishing with Mary Margaret's husband, Kevin.

"Why don't you let Nic come home with me and Shawn for playtime and dinner? I'll bring him home around eight."

Alison bit her lip. "I don't know. If Nic's with us...well, I don't feel so nervous."

Michelle touched Alison's hand. "Like I said, it's just dinner. And maybe you need a little time to find out how you really feel."

"If Nic's not there, it feels like a date," Alison admitted.

Michelle nodded. "I think it *is* a date, Ali."

"I don't feel ready for a date," Alison said, but even as she said the words she felt that maybe, just maybe, if it was a date with Jeremy, she might be ready.

Jeremy meandered through the aisles of the small grocery store, trying to find the ingredients he needed for the meal that night. Given that Estes Park was a not a big town, Jeremy had expected the shopping to be limited. He stopped for a moment to inspect his basket and deduce what else he needed.

When Alison told him that Nic would be having dinner with Michelle and Shawn—well, creating a delicious meal became that much more important. Jeremy was cooking for Alison, and everything needed to be perfect. He'd decided to make chicken vesuvio, a favorite dish of his and one he knew so well that he could probably make it in his sleep. And for dessert, he decided on another favorite of his—bread pudding. Bread pudding wasn't on the menu at Romano's, so Jeremy rarely made it. But whenever he was home visiting his mother, it was the one dessert she always requested and he was happy to oblige.

Once his grocery cart brimmed with chicken, olive oil, cloves of garlic, red potatoes, celery, carrots and white wine for cooking, he turned his attention to the necessary ingredients for his dessert. He picked up bread, eggs, brown sugar, and pecans—in case Alison didn't have any.

At the last minute, he decided to grab a bouquet of fresh flowers. He whipped over to the small selection and picked the bunch that looked the most vibrant and colorful.

Am I trying too hard? Am I making this into a date when it's just supposed to be two friends having dinner? Friends that just met a week ago...I keep forgetting that part. I feel like I've known Alison longer.

Standing in the check-out lane, Jeremy thought over the kiss they'd shared the night before. He had no doubt in his mind that that kiss had been building between them for days. But afterward, Alison had become flustered, apologizing and rushing back downstairs. He'd turned the lights off and made sure the doors were locked before heading upstairs, unsure about how Alison felt. And that morning before church, she'd acted as though nothing had happened.

But as someone who liked to be straightforward and clear about things, pretending something hadn't happened didn't work well for Jeremy. When Alison had told him that Nic was hanging out at a friend's house, Jeremy hoped that this would be the right opportunity for the two of them to talk, *really talk*, about what was going on between them.

Even if she says the kiss was a mistake and she's not interested in a relationship—I need to hear it from her. He would respect her feelings, of course. But he needed to know.

Jeremy felt his own feelings were just as jumbled. On one hand, he knew he'd never felt as connected and attracted to a woman as he did with Alison. On the other hand, he had a full life in Denver that he didn't plan to give up. So maybe any sort of relationship wasn't realistic.

Still, we need to talk this through. If that kiss told me anything, it's that we both wanted it. I'm not the only one feeling the attraction here.

When he got back to the B&B, Jeremy saw a note on the door from Alison that said she had gone for a walk and would be back soon. Jeremy felt relieved; he'd be able to get right to work in the kitchen without any interference.

He was already sautéing the chicken in olive oil when Alison walked through the open sliding door.

"It was a getting a little warm in here," Jeremy said apologetically.

"The autumn breeze is perfect. Keep the door open if you want. How about if I set the table for us? I was thinking we'd eat in the dining room tonight rather than the breakfast area."

"Sure," Jeremy agreed, his attention back on the chicken. "Alison," he turned back to her and motioned to the flowers on the counter. "Those are for you."

She smiled at him. "Thank you, Jeremy. You didn't have to do that."

"I wanted to."

Alison filled a vase with water and arranged the flowers, then disappeared into the dining room, and Jeremy exhaled with relief. He knew he could be a little antisocial when it came to working in the kitchen. He was used to being responsible for a kitchen filled with people and the only way to keep things running smoothly was order, structure and attention. He knew that whenever his sous chef, Margo, ran the Romano's kitchen for him, she tended to be more laid-back and allowed more joking and laughter. But Jeremy ran a tight kitchen.

He wasn't used to cooking in this kind of setting—alone with a woman. Not that he didn't like it; in fact, making chili with Alison had been an excellent experience for him.

But he took food seriously. As a chef, he wanted the dining experience to be something customers delighted in. And for this night, he wanted that especially for Alison.

Once he'd sautéed the potatoes, chicken and other vegetables, he arranged them in a casserole dish, then made the sauce. He tasted it then added a bit more seasoning and wine. Once it tasted the way he wanted it to, he poured the sauce over the chicken and vegetables and slid the pan into the oven. He took a few moments to clean his work station and prep for the dessert, enjoying the enticing smell of sautéed chicken and garlic that wafted through the kitchen.

A draft blew through the kitchen and Jeremy could tell that the temperature outside was dropping. He closed the sliding door and peeked into the dining room. Alison was nowhere to be found, but the table looked impressive. She'd brought out beautiful china, and two long-stemmed candles graced the center.

As Jeremy stood admiring the table, suddenly a rush of nerves hit him.

She's set the table for something special.
Nic isn't here.
This is a date.

Alison stared at herself in the mirror—the crease in her forehead, the dark circles under her eyes. She felt so much older than thirty-three. The loss of Connor had aged her. And with so many pressures swirling through her mind, she felt tired all of the time.

But not tonight.

Upstairs, Jeremy had prepared dinner for the two of them. She'd talked herself into setting the table with china her mother had given her. She rarely used it, except for special occasions. She hoped Jeremy didn't think she was silly—breaking out her special china for their meal together.

She felt *so* anxious. She'd gone for a walk after church, desperately needing to be alone with God. She'd walked to her favorite large rock by the river, sat down on it and absorbed the cool air while pouring out her heart to her heavenly Father.

After she'd set the table and headed downstairs for a few moments alone before dinner, Alison had slipped into her straight dark blue jeans and put on a black knit top with a wide collar, adding some white dangling earrings. She straightened her hair, and despite feeling borderline ridiculous, she'd added some mascara and lipstick. Because Nic was her primary company and he didn't care about mascara, she hardly ever took the time for makeup.

Looking in the mirror now, Alison was surprised by how she looked.

She hadn't wanted to dress up or even attempt to look pretty since Connor had died. She just couldn't imagine life without Connor, and dressing up for anything made it feel like she was moving on without him.

She felt a twinge of remorse for wanting to look nice for Jeremy.

Alison drew in a shaky breath.

Father, I know Connor loved me. And I loved him. And I know he's gone now and he—more than anyone—would want me to find happiness again. And I want to. This just feels scary to me.

She heard a knock at the top of the stairs.

"Alison?" Jeremy called down. "Dinner's ready."

"Coming!" Alison responded quickly. She took one more look in the mirror and prayed for peace. Words from a scripture verse entered her thoughts.

I will trust and not be afraid. For the Lord is my strength and my song.

She walked upstairs and breathed in the delicious scent.

"Mmm! What are we having?" she asked as she joined Jeremy in the dining room. He'd already served their dishes and lit the candles. The room looked incredibly romantic.

"We're having chicken vesuvio. I hope you enjoy it." Jeremy pulled out a chair for Alison, and she sat down, trying to ignore the butterflies in her stomach. Jeremy prayed over the meal, and Alison took note of how beautiful the dish in front of her looked, not to mention the mouthwatering aroma.

"Is this a specialty of yours?" she asked with a smile. Sitting across from her, Jeremy nodded.

"It's a favorite at Romano's."

"I'm going to have to drive down to Denver sometime and go to this famous restaurant."

Jeremy grinned. "I'd love that. I hope you and Nicholas will come and see me sometime."

Alison gulped. It felt like the conversation was jump-starting to discussing how they might still see each other after Jeremy left the B&B.

She took a bite and savored the taste. "Jeremy, you must know how delicious this is."

He just smiled. "I'm glad you like it."

"I can't believe you've been eating my meatloaf when you can cook like this."

Jeremy chuckled. "Don't forget, I've been to culinary school. And I think you're a great cook. Nicholas and I are both big fans."

That simple, sweet comment caused a swell in her throat. She appreciated that he continued to include Nicholas.

"Nicholas is everything to me," Alison said, her voice soft. Jeremy nodded with understanding.

"I know."

"If it hadn't been for him, I would have given up after losing Connor." Alison thought for a moment and amended her statement. "Well, if it hadn't been for Nicholas and Jesus. Both of them kept me going."

"What about…and, of course, you don't have to answer, I was just wondering, what are your plans for the house now?"

Alison took a sip of water and then cut another piece of chicken. "I'm not sure. I mean, I have lots of ideas for improvements, but then—you need funds for that kind of thing. And I have to be careful with how much I'm spending because we're not making that much right now. Like I said before, I'm hoping we'll get more guests this fall. In fact, I had two emails today with reservation requests. One from a young couple who want to come up the weekend after next and another for a family the following weekend."

"That's great!"

Alison nodded. "It's encouraging, that's for sure. But as I told my dad, I need to set a timeframe for myself. If things don't look any better in a few months, I think I need to start planning for a new career."

"What did you do before you and Connor bought the B&B?" Jeremy asked.

"I went to college, thinking I'd become an elementary teacher. But I never received my teaching certificate. By the time I graduated, I knew teaching wasn't for me, but it was too late to change my major. So I came home and worked in the elementary school library for a couple of years. And I was…you're going to laugh," Alison warned. Jeremy shook his head.

"I won't," he argued. She sighed.

"You will, but I'll tell you anyway. I was the school mascot."

Jeremy pressed his lips together to keep the smile from overtaking his face. "Which was?"

"A pinecone."

A burst of laughter escaped and then Jeremy coughed, obviously trying to stifle his laughter. But Alison just chuckled along with him.

"It's okay."

"So what brought an end to your days as a pinecone?" Jeremy asked. Suppressed laughter filled his eyes in a way that made Alison want to just stop talking and stare at him.

"Oh, um," she tried to organize her thoughts. "Well, I met Connor. He was a middle-school teacher for the same school district. He taught science. And we started dating soon after we met. I fell head over heels in love with him on our first date. We were married within six months. He'd always dreamed of owning his own business. We came up with the idea of buying a B&B and running it together. So we saved for a while, then I got pregnant with Nicholas. So our idea was put on hold for a couple of years. But after Nicholas turned three, we started dreaming again. And this time, we both were ready to make it happen. We found this place and took the plunge. We had to do some updating and a few renovations to make it suitable for a B&B—that mainly included redoing the basement, which was much more expensive that we had anticipated, and making a few changes to the kitchen. We added a few bathrooms upstairs. Then we started having guests.

"We loved it—Connor and me. It was everything we'd

hoped it would be. A lot of work, but so much fun. Unfortunately, after he passed, I couldn't do anything for months. There was no way I could entertain guests."

"That's understandable, Alison," Jeremy broke in gently.

She took another sip of water. "I suppose," she agreed, fiddling with the food on her plate. "But now—well, I finally made my way back to the land of the living, but I'm having a difficult time bringing this old place back to life."

"Do you have a website?" Jeremy asked.

"Of sorts—but it needs work, badly."

"What else does the place need?"

Alison wished they'd shift the conversation to a more interesting topic.

"Well, the exterior needs painting, as you've probably noticed. I'd like to spruce up the guest bedrooms and add some new furniture to the back deck. I wish I could make the first floor a little more updated and not so old-fashioned. And most of all, we need some marketing to draw people in."

"I see," Jeremy said. His mind seemed to be turning. "Well, hopefully we'll win the chili cook-off and you'll get some free publicity."

"That's what I'm hoping for," Alison nodded.

"And I hope you've saved room for dessert," Jeremy said, standing and clearing away their empty dishes.

"Of course! What did you make?"

"Bread pudding. My mother's favorite. Simple yet it always seems comforting and delicious to me."

Alison grinned. "Bread pudding is one of my all-time favorite desserts. Excellent choice." Alison stood. "I'll make the coffee and then let's have dessert in the living room."

By the time Jeremy and Alison were sitting in the living room, sipping coffee and eating their dessert, he felt ready to burst. No one had mentioned the kiss!

"How's the bread pudding?" he inquired, knowing he

needed to mention the kiss soon or he would go crazy, but still feeling nervous.

"Perfect. Much like everything about the meal tonight. And the company. Thank you, Jeremy."

Jeremy took a deep breath.

Now or never.

"So, about last night…" he began, slowly stirring his coffee. Even in the dim lighting, he could see a flush creep up Alison's neck.

"Right. About that," she said.

"I can't say I'm sorry for kissing you, Alison," Jeremy chose his words carefully. The light from the lamps illuminated the gleam in her eyes as she looked up at him.

"I can't say I'm sorry either, Jeremy."

"I'm pretty out of practice," he confessed. The corners of her lips tilted upward.

"That makes two of us."

"I like you, Alison." Jeremy looked right at her.

"You barely know me," she countered cautiously.

"I think I do. And I know I'd like to continue our friendship, even after I leave for Denver."

"I want that, too," she said. "But I'm not sure I'm ready for this."

"I don't want to rush you into anything. And since I'll be in Denver and you'll be up here, I'm not even sure of how things will work out. If I lived here—"

"But you don't."

Jeremy paused. He stood up and moved to sit next to Alison on the sofa, facing her.

"No, I don't. But I care about you. And about Nicholas."

"I know you do. But I have to be really careful. Especially when it comes to Nicholas."

"I understand."

Jeremy watched as Alison twisted her hands. He could almost see her mentally wrestling with her words.

"I like you, too, Jeremy. I really do."

Jeremy looked at her. Alison's blond hair was soft and silky. Her brown eyes were filled with concern and maybe a hint of yearning. It was enough. He took her hand in his and kissed her again.

"So let's try. That's all I'm asking. Denver isn't that far. I can come up to visit. You can drive down to the city. I have friends you could stay with. Just give me a chance, Ali," he said. Their foreheads touched and Jeremy kept his eyes closed as he waited for her answer. He'd never wanted anything quite so much as he wanted a *yes* from Alison Taylor at this moment.

She exhaled, staying close to him.

"All right, Jeremy Mitchell. You win. I'll try."

Chapter 13

"Nic, you need your jacket! It's going to be chilly today!" Alison yelled from the top of the stairs down to the basement.

"Okay, Mom!" In less than a minute Nicholas was taking the stairs two at a time up to the front door. He dashed past Alison, his red jacket just a flash in her line of view.

Satisfied, she turned back and walked to the kitchen where Jeremy was loading up a large box with their chili and supplies.

"We're set," he said, lifting the box. "Are we taking my truck?"

Alison shook her head. "My SUV has more room. You can slide the box into the back. I'll grab a jacket and meet you out there."

She turned off the lights and slipped into a windbreaker, hoping the wind would die down. The crisp cool air and sunshine were a nice blend, but the wind in the mountains could get intense and Alison was picturing bowls of chili flying off the table. She locked the front door and jumped into the driver's seat. The smell of spicy ground beef made its way all through the car.

"I'm hungry," Nicholas said, and Alison laughed.

"You just had breakfast! Wait till we get to the festival. Every booth is going to have good food, and I have a feeling you're going to want to try everything."

"I can't wait! You're going to have so much fun at the

festival, Jeremy," Nicholas chattered. "Really. It's, like, the most fun *ever*."

Jeremy grinned. "I believe you, kiddo."

Alison glanced sideways at Jeremy, and he winked at her. She wasn't sure whether it was Jeremy's presence or the chill in the air that caused tingles to shoot through her. She was pretty sure it was the former. The past few days had been better than she expected. The fact that she and Jeremy had acknowledged that they liked each other and were interested in a relationship had resulted in a more relaxed atmosphere.

Jeremy had talked Alison into going fishing with him Monday, so they'd spent the day at the river, with her learning to cast his fly rod and the two of them having a picnic by the water. Tuesday morning her dad had driven over, and he and Jeremy had fished for a few hours before coming back to the house. Then the three of them had sat down to a lunch of potato soup and tuna melts. Alison was both pleased and surprised by how well her dad and Jeremy seemed to get along.

After Nic got home on Tuesday, the three of them went for a hike, then came home to beef stew that had simmered all day in Alison's crockpot. Wednesday Jeremy had gone with her to serve lunch at the soup kitchen. She hadn't told anyone she was bringing him, so the sight of him caused quite a stir among the ladies at River Community. Alison had enjoyed every minute serving up soup and sandwiches alongside him.

Thursday the festival began, but Alison and Jeremy were busy preparing for the chili cook-off on Friday. Jeremy had needed to go into town for more ingredients for the chili, so they'd gone to the Donut Haus for pastries before spending some time shopping in Estes Park, navigating through the hustle and bustle of the opening festivities. The town was already bursting with people. The festival always seemed to bring in more tourists. Alison wished that had resulted in a few more visitors at the B&B.

The challenge of finding a parking space on Friday morning had Alison frustrated before they even unloaded their supplies.

"Ali," Jeremy said smoothly. "We're early. We have plenty of time," he reminded her. She finally found a spot and Nicholas bounced out of the car. Alison followed him to the back of the SUV, where Jeremy was unloading the box.

"Remember, Nic. We're meeting Miss Michelle and Shawn here, then you're going to hang out with them for a couple of hours. And I expect you—"

"To listen and be respectful and stay with Miss Michelle. I know!" Nic repeated. Alison stopped. She reached out and quickly bestowed a kiss on the top of Nic's head.

"I love you," she said. Nic gave her a quick hug.

"Love you, too. And tonight we're watching the fireworks together, right?" he asked.

"Right," Jeremy confirmed. Michelle and Shawn showed up and within seconds, the boys' excitement level skyrocketed.

"Are you sure you can handle them?" Alison murmured doubtfully. Michelle smiled.

"Not a problem. You two go win this cook-off."

"We'll try. Thanks, friend."

"Have fun! Save me a bowl!" Michelle called out as she took off after the boys who were already ahead of her. Alison took in the setting before her. Golden leaves flittered down the street like a perfect autumn parade. Banners hung over Main Street and people meandered around every corner of the town. The sounds of talking and laughter drifted from all directions. Horse-drawn wagons lined the street for hayrides. The town look festive and inviting with strategically placed round orange pumpkins, barrels of red apples and bales of hay. Alison drank in the beauty of the mountains, majestic and regal, overlooking the lively town.

She felt a familiar sense come over her—a sense of belonging, of contentment. She was reminded all over again of how much she loved living in this small, mountain town.

"Ali!" Alison turned at the sound of Jeremy calling her name. He waved her over toward the booth. Alison waved back, thinking that the sight of Jeremy Mitchell wearing an apron and stirring a big pot of chili made the festival even more exciting to her.

Jeremy tasted the chili, trying to temper his anxiety. His competitive nature, coupled with the importance of winning those marketing opportunities for Alison, made this chili cook-off a priority for him. As he glanced around at the competition, he felt a bit more worried. The blustery breeze carried the aroma of chili throughout the booths, and by the incredible smells, Jeremy had a feeling some of the folks around him really knew what they were doing. Particularly the lumberjack next to them who kept reminding people that he was the reigning champion.

"Don't worry," Alison whispered, following Jeremy's gaze. "I think ours is better."

Jeremy's anxiety lessened for a moment as he looked at Alison. With a blond braid over each of her shoulders, a red plaid shirt under her light brown jacket and caramel-colored cowboy boots, she looked charming, not to mention absolutely beautiful. It occurred to him that she was in her element, completely at home in this small town.

He envied her. As much as he enjoyed the surge of energy when it came to cooking for a restaurant like Romano's, so much about this small-town life appealed to him. The space to breathe. The mountains that left him in awe. The woman next to him. Since their conversation Sunday evening, Alison had seemed to warm up to him, opening herself to the possibility of a relationship between them, despite the distance factor.

"Here come the judges!" Alison squealed. Jeremy snapped

back to attention and divvied out a small bowl for each of the four judges. He studied their reactions. Although they each strived to be impassive, Jeremy had cooked for people long enough to recognize the small signs that told him they liked it. The second spoonful, the lick of the lips. As they marked down their notes and moved to the next booth, Jeremy let out a deep breath.

"Do you think they liked it?" Alison asked, her voice unsure.

"I think so," he whispered back.

An hour later, Alison and Jeremy stood with the other contestants as they waited for the announcement. They'd spent the past fifty minutes doling out chili and talking with the people who stopped by their booth. Michelle had brought the boys, who'd devoured their bowls, then raced off for more fun. Jeremy reached down and took her hand in his. She held it tightly.

"Well, first of all, the other judges and I want to say that this year the chili competition was phenomenal. We've never had such a difficult time deciding! Everyone excelled. We'll start with the second runner-up: Christina and Adam Sanchez!"

Everyone clapped for the happy couple, who received a ribbon and a fifty-dollar certificate.

"First runner-up goes to Mike Benson!"

Jeremy recognized the lumberjack, and last year's champion, as he made his way forward and accepted his one-hundred-dollar gift certificate with a bit of a grumble.

Jeremy held his breath.

"And first prize goes to Jeremy Mitchell and Alison Taylor!" Jeremy let out a whoop and Alison clapped her hands exuberantly.

"We won!" she shouted. He picked her up and swung her around before planting her back on her feet. Her eyes shone as she looked up at him. Without hesitating, Jeremy kissed her.

When he let go of her, his eyes went directly behind her, where Michelle, Shawn, Nicholas and Alison's parents were standing, mouths wide open in shock. Jeremy froze. Alison turned, her eyes following his, and she paled at the sight of Nic and her parents.

"Come on up here, you two!" the judge called out. Jeremy tugged at Alison's hand and led her to the stage, where they were presented with a blue ribbon, a $500 check and a stack of cards and certificates for Alison to follow up on those marketing options. But the smile on her face now seemed forced, and he knew she was thinking of Nicholas.

Once the pomp and circumstance of the moment was over, they made their way back to the dispersing crowd and found Nicholas, who was being uncharacteristically quiet. Worry filled Jeremy.

Why did I kiss her like that in front of a crowd of people! I hope Nic isn't too upset. She hadn't mentioned to Nic that they were anything more than friends. He was probably completely freaked out. And Jolene and Eli looked beyond shocked. He had a feeling he might have lost all the headway he'd made with Eli on Tuesday.

"Hey, buddy," Jeremy said to Nicholas. "Now that the cook-off is over, we can go on a hayride. Do you want to?"

"Um, Grandpa said he'll take me," Nicholas said without looking at Jeremy. He went and stood between his grandparents, whom Jeremy intentionally avoided eye contact with at that moment.

"That's right. We'll go see if there's one ready now. Ali, do you want to come?" Eli asked, his tone restrained. Alison looked at Jeremy.

"Absolutely, you should go," he said. "Leave me the SUV keys and I'll load up our supplies and meet up with you guys after."

She looked torn, but she agreed, handed over the keys and then took off with her parents and Nicholas. Jeremy watched them go.

"Need some help?" Jeremy turned in surprise at the sound of Michelle's voice. He hadn't realized that she and Shawn were still there.

"No, that's okay. Thank you for offering," Jeremy replied, noticing the dejected sound of his voice but unable to do anything about it.

"We don't mind, right, Shawn?" Michelle said lightly. Shawn ran ahead and started stacking up the paper bowls. "So, you seem to really like my friend Alison. Am I right?" Michelle asked as they walked slowly toward the booth. Jeremy sighed.

"Yeah, I do. But I shouldn't have kissed her like that. It didn't even occur to me that Nic would be watching."

"One thing you should know about dating a single mom—you *always* need to consider that her child might be watching and how it could affect him."

Jeremy nodded in solemn agreement.

"But I wouldn't worry too much. Ali needs to talk to Nic. She probably should have done so earlier because it looks like she likes you as much as you like her." Michelle gently elbowed Jeremy in the arm. "This just sped up the conversation. But once they talk things through, it will be okay. Nic is a terrific kid. But he's still just an eight-year-old who's lost his dad and now might have to adjust to his mom dating. And that's a lot for any child to go through."

"You're right. And I wish they hadn't lost Connor. I know he was a great father and husband."

"He was," Michelle confirmed. "But that doesn't mean Alison won't ever find love again. It can happen," Michelle said with the hint of a smile.

"I don't think her parents are on board with her dating anyone. And now Nicholas might be against it, too."

Michelle shrugged and stacked rolled napkins in the cardboard box. "Alison has to search her heart and do what's right for her. She's a woman of faith. I know she'll trust the Lord to lead her. Everything's a little more complicated when there's a child to consider. Alison's a good mother."

"She's an incredible mother," Jeremy said, his words sincere. He placed the large cooking pot in the box and noticed Michelle studying him.

"If you haven't noticed already, her life is firmly rooted here. She loves living in the mountains, Jeremy. I don't know if she's told you, but she lived in Denver all through college, and city life just wasn't for her. She couldn't wait to get back to the mountains. It's part of who she is."

He closed up the box. "I can tell. So, are you saying you don't think there's a chance that things will work out between us?"

Michelle shook her head. "No, I'm not saying that. I absolutely believe that with God, anything is possible."

Jeremy felt a surge of hope at that reminder. "I believe that, too."

Michelle and Shawn said goodbye and Jeremy loaded up the SUV, then went strolling down Main Street in search of Alison and Nicholas. He walked down the sidewalk, admiring the already snow-capped mountains in the distance and the host of yellow- and red-leafed trees lining the streets. He zipped up his vest as the temperature lowered, then stopped to buy five candy apples from a street vendor.

He made his way to the line for hayrides and waited for Alison and Nicholas to return, a prayer filling his thoughts.

God, maybe we're off to a rocky start, but the feelings I have for Alison are so strong—I'm not ready to give up. Help me convince her parents I only want what's best for her. Help me assure Nicholas that his feelings matter to me, too. And please, give me some idea how to make this work despite the fact that my life is established in Denver and Alison's is set in Estes Park.

Chapter 14

Alison sat squished between her mother and Nicholas on the wagon as they made the turn and headed back toward Main Street. Nicholas had rebounded somewhat; at least he seemed to be having fun again after the awkwardness at the cook-off.

How could I have let that happen? I'm getting carried away by this crush. So is Jeremy. I should have been more guarded. Now instead of easing Nic into the idea of my dating, he's thrown in headfirst by seeing his mother kiss someone! Good grief!

"Alison?" her mother said in a quiet voice. "Are you all right?"

Alison felt the wagon roll to a stop. "I'm okay, Mom. Really."

"I have to admit I'm a little worried about—"

"I'm not ready to talk about it. When I have a moment alone with him, I'll talk to Nicholas about everything. Right now, just please understand and don't mention it," Alison said in rushed sentences that, she hoped, communicated decisiveness.

"Of course, dear." Her mother nodded.

As they filed off the wagon, Alison was relieved when she saw Jeremy waiting for them. She'd felt a bit conflicted, hoping he'd find them, and at the same time, hoping he'd stay away. But when she saw him, her heart did that pitter-patter thing it seemed to do every time she was near him. And she couldn't help feeling glad he'd sought them out.

He held out his hand to help her off the wagon. She took his hand but dropped it quickly once she was down. Nic jumped down after her.

"I have candy apples! Anyone want one?" Jeremy announced. Nicholas nodded.

"Sure! I want one. Can I have one, Mom?"

Alison nodded and took one for herself. She and Jeremy fell in step behind Nicholas and her parents.

"I'm sorry about earlier," Jeremy whispered. Alison kept her eyes on Nicholas.

"I know. It's okay. I mean, I think it will be okay. I'll talk to Nic later."

"Do you want me to talk to him?"

"No, I need to."

They walked down Main Street, stopping at booths along the way before making their way to the park, where people were congregating to watch the evening fireworks display. Alison went back to the car to retrieve a picnic blanket and a heavier jacket for Nicholas, and the family claimed a spot on the open lawn.

They sat together on Alison's old patchwork quilt, and as dusk fell over the town, the sky lit up like wildflowers. Along with her parents and Nicholas and Jeremy, Alison oohed and ahhed over the bursts of color exploding above them. The discomfort from the cook-off seemed to have passed, and Alison breathed easier. They drove home after the fireworks with Alison and Jeremy quiet in the front seat as Nicholas slept in the back.

Alison woke Nicholas once they arrived and directed him into the house and downstairs; Jeremy waved her on, assuring her that he'd unload the car, lock up the house and turn off the lights. With no argument, Alison tucked Nicholas into bed and pulled on her pajamas before crawling into bed herself. She lay awake, exhausted yet unable to turn her mind off from the day's events.

Saturday morning Jeremy woke up tired after a restless night. He stretched and walked to the windows overlooking the woods and river and a prayer filled his thoughts.

Father, I know I'm leaving today. I know I have to go home. But I feel so torn, leaving Alison and Nicholas. I want to be here. I want to keep getting to know Alison. I want to take Nicholas fishing. I want to enjoy the golden leaves and the cold rushing water and the peace that I've experienced here.

But I have to go.

Jeremy sighed and turned from the window. He packed his suitcase and then texted Leo to let him know he'd be back in town that evening. He made his bed and straightened the bathroom; he didn't want to leave a mess for Alison. Then he headed downstairs.

He could smell red peppers and fried potatoes before he reached the kitchen. He walked through the open entryway and smiled at the sight of Nicholas at the table, playing games on his mom's cell phone, and Alison at the stove, frying hash browns.

"Good morning!" Jeremy said as he made his way to the coffeepot and poured himself a mug of the strong, dark blend. Alison smiled at him warmly and Nicholas looked up with a grin.

"Hi, Jeremy," he said before looking back down at the game. Jeremy wondered if Alison had already talked with Nicholas about the impromptu kiss he'd witnessed at the cook-off. The tension from the night before seemed to have lifted.

"Breakfast is almost ready," Alison announced. "Jeremy, could you grab the plates?"

Something tightened in Jeremy at her request—the feeling that he was no longer a guest but a part of the family, the sense that he belonged there.

Nicholas begrudgingly set aside the game so he and Jeremy could set out plates and forks and napkins. Alison placed dishes of seasoned hash browns, scrambled eggs and biscuits on the table, and the three of them sat down to eat.

"Jeremy, would you pray for us?" she asked.

His heart tugged again. He looked down at his plate—Alison and Nicholas on either side of him—and swallowed hard before praying. A strong sentiment covered him. A feeling of *family*.

He found the words to pray, and then the three of them dug into breakfast. He and Nic complimented Alison on the meal and all three chatted about the fun of the festival and the thrill of winning the chili cook-off. As breakfast wound down, Alison sipped her coffee and peered over at Jeremy.

"What's your plan, Jeremy? I know you said you were leaving today."

Nicholas's eyes darted to Jeremy.

He cleared his throat before answering. "I am. I started packing this morning. I have a few more things to pack—I need to put together my fishing gear—and I'll be ready to go. I hope you both know how much I've enjoyed staying here. I'm going to miss you two," Jeremy said, working hard to keep his tone light.

"We're going to miss you too—aren't we, Mom?"

Jeremy's eyes zeroed in on Alison. Her mouth opened and closed once before finally answering.

"Yes. We definitely will," she said. "But I'm sure we'll see Jeremy again."

Their eyes met.

Across from him at the table, Alison, in gray stretch pants and a light pink hoodie, sat with her blond hair tied in a knot at the nape of her neck. They just looked at each other for a moment and Jeremy's heart pounded. Then Nic stepped away from the table to get more juice, and the moment was over.

Once the dishes were cleared away, Jeremy went upstairs to finish packing. He stacked his luggage by the front door and took his fishing gear out to the truck. He wanted one last trek out to the river. The leaves crunched under his boots as he walked from the back deck toward the water.

"Jeremy!"

He turned at the sound of Nicholas calling his name.

"Hey, buddy. What's up?"

"Can I walk with you to the river? Mom said it's okay."

Jeremy motioned for him to join him. "Then come on down."

Nicholas ran to catch up with him and they both walked to the riverbank.

"I'm going to miss this river," Jeremy said as he looked at the water running over the rocks.

"My mom told me that she likes you," Nicholas said in a quiet voice.

Jeremy coughed. "Oh. Did she?"

Nicholas looked at him with interest. "Do you like her?"

Jeremy nodded. "Very much. How do you feel about that?"

Nicholas looked down at his shoes. "Kinda weird."

They were both silent for a moment. "Would you be okay with me seeing you and your mom again sometime? Like if I came back for a visit? Or if you two drove down to Denver to visit me?" Jeremy asked.

Nicholas nodded. "Yeah. I think that would be okay."

"I think your mom is really special," Jeremy said.

"Yeah, she is," Nicholas agreed.

"But I also think you're really special, Nic."

Nicholas looked up at him.

"You do?"

"Definitely. And I'm glad to have you as my friend."

Nicholas seemed to think that over for a second. "I'm glad to have you as my friend, too."

"Maybe you could text me sometime. Let me know how you're doing," Jeremy suggested. Nicholas nodded.

"Sure. And you can text me, too, or call me. Grandpa told me that he was going to keep fly-fishing with me. Next time you come, we can go fishing again."

"That's sounds great."

Jeremy and Nicholas both looked behind them at the sound of more footsteps walking down the path.

"Grandpa!" Nicholas exclaimed. He raced up the path. Eli stopped for a quick hug.

"Your mom needs your help, Nic. Head on back to the house for me, son."

Nicholas took off toward the house and Eli walked down to where Jeremy stood. Jeremy felt a sense of trepidation, but he stifled that and managed a smile.

"Eli! I didn't know you were coming by."

"Jolene and I wanted to come over and see you off."

"Well, that was sure kind of you."

"And I wanted to thank you for the fly-fishing lesson on Tuesday. I enjoyed our time together."

"So did I. I hope we get the chance to do it again sometime."

Eli folded his arms across his chest. "Do you have any plans to come back to Estes Park in the near future?"

Jeremy smiled. "I'd like to. But my schedule can be pretty demanding. So it may be a little while before I make it back."

"I see," Eli said, his tone deepening. "I want to talk to you about something else—we might as well just acknowledge the fact that you seem to really like my daughter."

Jeremy swallowed. "Yes, I do. We're friends. If I lived here, I'd like to start dating her and spend more time with her. That will be difficult because I live in Denver. But I don't mind telling you I hope that she and I keep in touch."

"I appreciate you being honest with me. I hope you don't mind if I'm equally honest—Alison has endured a lot of heartache. You know that. I also know that it's completely reasonable to think that she might want to remarry one day. But she has a lot of pressure on her right now to make this business a success. And it took a long time for her to have enough space from her grief where she could function. I'd hate to see her heartbroken again."

A sharp wind passed through the trees, rustling leaves and branches. The sound filled Jeremy's ears and the cool gust gave him a chill.

The Lord will guide you always.

Jeremy looked at Eli. "I understand and respect your feelings. I can assure you that hurting Alison is the *last* thing I'd ever want to do. I'm leaving today. She and I plan to keep in contact, but I don't know where that will lead. All I can tell you is that I care about Alison and Nicholas. I feel fortunate to have met them. And I trust the Lord to guide me…and Alison."

Eli nodded slowly. "I'm relieved to hear that. I suppose that means we can part as friends."

Jeremy shook Eli's hand warmly. "Thank you for that, Eli."

"Thank *you* for all you've done during your time here. Nicholas told me you've helped out around the house—and you didn't have to stay for the festival. I know you did it to help Ali, and that means a lot to all of us. So I look forward to seeing you the next time you're in our neck of the woods."

The two men walked side by side back up to the house, and Jeremy released a sigh of relief.

Chapter 15

Alison stood in the foyer of her home as her parents and Nicholas said goodbye to Jeremy, her heart pounding.

I don't want him to leave.

But he's leaving. He has to. I knew this was coming.

The Lord is my strength.

After the goodbyes were said, Jeremy looked at her over Nicholas's head.

"Ali, would you walk me out?"

She nodded, moving past her parents. "Of course."

"I'll come!" Nicholas announced. Alison looked at her mom.

"You stay with us, Nic. Let's go get lunch started," her mother said firmly. Alison mouthed *Thank you* to her mother, and Nic was steered back down the hallway by Alison's parents.

Jeremy and Alison walked out onto the front porch, and she closed the door behind them.

"I have your money," Alison said, holding out the $250 that was Jeremy's share of the prize money.

He shook his head. "There's no way I'm taking that. Going to the cook-off was fun for me. These past two weeks have been a wonderful experience. That money is yours, Alison."

"But—"

Jeremy placed one finger to her lips. "No 'buts.' Going to the cook-off with you was my pleasure. Consider the money payment for the many extra meals you cooked for me while I was here."

Alison closed her fingers over the bills and nodded. "Thank you."

"Thank *you* for being such a lovely hostess," Jeremy said.

Alison smiled. "It's my job."

Jeremy shook his head. "I feel like you let me be part of your family for the past two weeks. Thank you for the meals, and thank you for the time you spent with me."

Alison felt a lump rise in her throat. "Thanks for being my friend. I needed one."

Jeremy took her hand in his. "I want to keep being your friend, Alison."

"That's going to happen. I want to keep being your friend, too."

"So you talked to Nicholas. How did that go?"

Alison shrugged. "Fairly well. I just explained to him that you and I want to keep getting to know each other. I think as long as he and I are open and honest with each other—and he knows he can talk to me and let me know whatever he's feeling—we're going to be okay. It's obvious how much Nic misses Connor. But I know he's enjoyed having you here. He's going to miss you."

"I'm going to miss him too." Jeremy stood still as Alison took one step closer to him. "And you, Ali. You know I'm going to miss you."

She nodded. "We'll stay in touch. We'll see what happens."

Jeremy kissed her, and Alison wished she could freeze the moment in time. But she'd lived long enough to know that moments came and went. Even if she wanted to hold on to this one. Even if she wanted to hold on to this man. She looked at Jeremy, with his short blond hair and easy smile.

God, why did you bring him into my life? He's leaving. He's not here to stay.

"So…you'll call me soon, right?" she said. Jeremy placed one hand on her shoulder and looked right into her eyes.

"I promise."

Alison stood in the driveway and watched until Jeremy's truck vanished from sight. She crossed her arms tightly in front of her. The chilly wind blew a swirl of leaves around the circular driveway. Alison tried to decipher her feelings. Lonely? Maybe. Saddened by Jeremy's leaving? Of course.

I guess my tiny glimpse at romance has ended. It's back to the real world for me. Back to mounting bills and a host of responsibilities she had to juggle all by herself. It had been so nice to have someone to share life with, even just for a few days. *But he's gone now.*

Her thoughts overwhelmed her and she shifted to prayer. *Father, it's You and me again. And my focus has to be on saving this business, if that's even possible. Christmas. That's the deadline I'm setting for myself. If we're still consistently losing money by Christmas, I need to sell and do something different. Either move in with my parents or find an apartment for Nicholas and myself.*

For some reason, the thought didn't bring with it the devastation that she normally felt. Turning around, Alison took in the full view of the B&B.

She could see Connor clearly in her mind's eye, picking her up and carrying her into the B&B right after they'd purchased it. She'd laughed that day and told him that crossing the threshold was for newlyweds. He'd kicked open the door and carried her inside, kissing her soundly and telling her that he wanted to cross this threshold with as much excitement as a newlywed couple.

Alison let the memory drift away, thankful for it, yet overtaken with thoughts of her present situation. Jeremy's kiss still lingered on her lips. She tried to hold off any tears.

She put her hands on her hips. *It's time to get to work saving the Mountain View Bed & Breakfast.*

* * *

Jeremy tied a red bandanna around his forehead and then reached for his apron. He'd made it back in time to run the Romano's kitchen that Saturday night. Walking through the kitchen as the staff prepped for dinner, Jeremy's emotions seemed to be on conflicting rollercoasters. On one hand, he kept thinking of Alison and Nicholas, wondering what they were doing that evening and wishing he was at the B&B with them. On the other hand, he was already feeling energized by the buzz of the restaurant. It was Saturday night; that meant, without a doubt, the kitchen would be busy. The Romano's on Fifteenth Street in downtown Denver was an increasingly popular venue.

The staff had welcomed Jeremy back warmly, asking about his vacation and whether he'd enjoyed the time away. Leo had come in to welcome him back, then left shortly for the Franklin Street Romano's location to stand in for a cook who'd called in sick. It had been a typical Saturday night, and by the time Jeremy walked out to his car, he could feel his shoulders aching. He drove home without turning the radio on, glad for the silence.

On Sunday, he took his time before attending the second service at his church. He sat alone in the middle of a crowd of people, barely singing along. He then listened to the pastor's message.

He missed the warmth of Alison's little church in the mountains and wondered if they'd be having a potluck again.

Get a grip, he scolded himself. *You're like a sentimental teenager home from camp. This is your life. Deal with it.*

After church, he stuck his hands in his pockets and walked through the parking lot toward his truck.

"Jeremy!"

He stopped at the sight of Ethan and Isabella Carter. They usually attended the Saturday night service, so Jeremy rarely saw them on Sunday mornings.

"Hey, guys!" he said, glad to see his friends. Ethan hugged him and Isabella just grinned at him over the top of their swaddled daughter's head.

"How's Layla doing?" Jeremy asked, leaning in for a peek.

"Still bald," Isabella answered dryly. "How is it that Leo has a son with hair like a lion, and I have a daughter without even peach fuzz?"

Ethan and Jeremy laughed. "It'll grow, Isa," Ethan assured her. "I mean, look at her mother. I'm sure Layla's hair will be beautiful. One day. Maybe not this year. But eventually."

Isabella shook back her own thick, wavy brown hair.

"Let's hope. So, Jeremy, want to come over for lunch? Are you on the schedule tonight?" she asked.

He nodded. "I'm cooking tonight. But lunch sounds great. I'll meet you guys at your place." He jumped back into his truck and drove to Ethan and Isabella's home in the city. He parked on the street and walked up the narrow sidewalk to their modest, two-story home. The door swung open and Isabella waved him in.

"Come in, but don't make a peep. Layla just fell asleep." Isabella paused. "Did that just rhyme?"

Jeremy smiled and followed Isabella down the hallway to the kitchen.

"We're taking advantage of the last few days of sunshine before the weather gets even more unpredictable than it is now. Ethan's grilling kabobs," Isabella told him. The two of them joined Ethan on the back porch. Isabella motioned for Jeremy to sit across from the glowing fire pit in the center of the stone porch. The fire pit reminded him of roasting marshmallows with Nicholas.

"So tell us all about your trip. Did you actually do any fishing? I heard there might have been some romance," Isa said with a wink. Jeremy glared at Ethan, but Ethan just shrugged.

"She's impossible to keep things from. Sorry, man. She basically interrogated me after our phone conversation."

"The B&B is run by Alison Taylor and her son, Nicholas," Jeremy told them both. "Her husband died two years ago of lymphoma."

Isabella frowned. "Oh, I'm sorry to hear that. How's she holding up after something like that?"

Jeremy sipped the soda that Ethan had given him. "She's more capable than most."

After a moment of quiet, Isabella rolled her eyes. "More capable than most? That's all you have to say? Really? Spill, Jeremy."

"I happen to think that's a great compliment. But fine… she's really pretty. And she's a great mother. Nicholas is a cool kid, inquisitive, respectful. I taught him to fly-fish. I taught both of them, actually. Oh, and Ali's dad, too. The chili cook-off was a success. We won the blue ribbon. I'd forgotten how much fun those competitions can be. Ali was so thrilled. I met her parents and her friends from church. They have a great community of folks up there. And the scenery was incredible. The B&B is right on the river. It needs some work. I'm hoping to help out with that, if I can. Like I said, Alison is really capable. But she's been through a lot."

Jeremy stopped at the stunned looks on Ethan and Isabella's faces.

"What?"

"Nothing," Isabella said. "It's just…I didn't realize that it was so serious."

"Serious?" Jeremy laughed uncomfortably. "I just met her. Why would you say that?"

Ethan gave him an almost pitiful look. "Because it's as clear as day that you *really* like this woman."

Jeremy didn't answer. He looked back at the fire pit. "I guess I do."

"Hey, that's a good thing, Jeremy," Isabella said gently.

"She's…you know, she still misses her husband. And she's got Nicholas, and she's really protective of him. And then there's the distance factor."

"Oh, Jeremy. You know God can work all that out, right? If you have feelings for Alison, you need to do something about it," Isa said.

"Well, I kissed her," Jeremy confessed. Ethan and Isabella both had eyes the size of golf balls.

"What?" Isa echoed. Ethan gave Jeremy a high five. Jeremy laughed, enjoying their shocked expressions.

"So…you *are* serious about this," Ethan said, taking a seat next to Isabella.

"I'm not sure how things will play out. She's really rooted in her community up there. I don't think she'd ever want to move. And you both know how much I love working at Romano's. But Alison is…I don't know how to explain it. I don't want to give up on her."

Isabella and Ethan exchanged a knowing glance.

"Don't do that, you two."

"Don't do what?" Ethan asked.

"That annoying thing that couples do—have an entire dialogue about the person across from them without saying anything."

Isabella chuckled. "Okay. Here's what we do. We start praying for God to work this out. If Alison and Nicholas mean this much to you, then we totally agree that you shouldn't give up on her." Isabella suddenly squealed and clapped her hands. "This is going to be so fun!"

"What is your wife talking about?" Ethan shook his head.

"I've almost given up trying to understand her. But I have a feeling she means that it's going to be fun to watch God work in your life, Jeremy."

Chapter 16

"What do you mean it will take six weeks?" Alison echoed, her arms folded across her chest. The guy at the desk in front of her typed another line on his computer before looking up.

"I mean the ad for the B&B won't go in the magazine for almost six weeks. We do our layouts months in advance. We did know this was coming, of course, when we signed up to be part of the free marketing for the cook-off winner. So we reserved space for an ad in our November issue. Think on the bright side! The ad will be out mid-November; that might give you a boost for December."

Alison took a breath.

He's right. It's free marketing regardless. I was hoping to see results sooner, but beggars can't be choosers, I guess.

"Okay. The list of marketing plugs includes online publicity. What will that look like?"

"Well, we will post an ad on our website, of course, featuring the B&B. But if I were you, I'd offer some sort of discount to get people's attention. Like 30 percent off for a three-day stay, or two free nights if someone sends you a referral. Maybe you could do something special for Christmas. The online ad or coupon will run for all of November and into the beginning of December so that could work well for you. But I need to know ASAP. Like yesterday. So come up with something and email it to me by tomorrow."

Alison blew out a huff of air. "By tomorrow. No problem."

The guy didn't seem to comprehend the sarcasm in her voice.

Just as well. It's not his fault. I'm just not good at coming up with ideas on the spot like this. I wish Jeremy were here.

Alison stepped out of the small building and made her way across the street. The newspaper was also running an ad for the B&B, and she'd brought photos and a write-up for them. She sure hoped this brought in more than a few customers. It would be so nice to have a full house for once and get caught up on bills without dipping into the insurance money again.

Alison had one more stop to make after the newspaper office. She rushed to one of the local travel agencies that was going to promote her B&B in an email blast to their online subscribers.

Afterward, she walked down the sidewalk back to her car. Her cell buzzed and she answered it.

"Ali! It's Michelle! Did I tell you that I'm painting the kitchen? I'm up to my chin in paint, so could you pick up Shawn from school for me when you get Nic?"

"Of course," Alison agreed. "I can take him home with me for dinner if you want me to."

"No need. I've got a lasagna in the oven. Why don't you and Nic join us for dinner when you bring Shawn home?"

The idea sounded perfect to Alison. She could brainstorm marketing ideas with Michelle over dinner.

She checked her watch, then headed to the school to pick up the boys. She was looking forward to a fun and productive evening.

Once they'd finished a lively dinner with the boys talking nonstop and Michelle and Alison discussing Michelle's home improvements and Ali's marketing possibilities, the boys were parked at the small kitchen island doing homework. Alison and Michelle sat on the back patio with a mug of hot tea each.

"So how did it go with that couple last weekend?" Michelle asked.

"Fine. They weren't at the house that much. I think they did a lot of sightseeing around town. We're supposed to have a family arrive on Friday night, staying till Sunday. After that, I've got nothing."

Michelle sipped her tea. "You'll have more guests closer to the holidays, I'm sure. Once the ads come out in the paper and wherever else. It's going to get better, Alison."

Alison stirred her tea and just nodded in silent agreement, although she struggled to believe it.

"Jeremy?" Michelle asked with a hint of a smile.

The right corner of Alison's mouth tilted upward. "He's called a couple of times. And he texts Nicholas on my phone, which thrills Nic, of course. We've emailed a few times too. I miss him."

"When do you think you might see him again?"

"Well, near the end of October Nancy, my friend from college, is getting married. The wedding is in Denver and I was already planning to go. So while Nicholas and I are in town for the wedding, we're going to get together with Jeremy. He's arranging for us to stay the night with some friends of his."

"Well, that sounds fun," Michelle said with a smile.

Alison cupped her hands around the warm mug. "I think so, too."

She thought of Jeremy and wondered if he missed her as much as she missed him.

"This is incredible, Jeremy," Leo Romano said, lifting the fork again to his lips to taste the sirloin marsala dish that Jeremy had created.

"I was thinking we could use it as the special next weekend. What do you think?" Jeremy asked.

"Absolutely. We'll put it on the specials board next Friday and I'll make sure we've ordered enough sirloin. The steak is cooked to perfection. Good job," Leo said, wiping his mouth with a cloth napkin and then cutting another piece of beef. "Go ahead," he motioned to the skillet on the stove. "Don't let this kind of meal go to waste."

Jeremy stood up from where they were sitting at the large island in the Romano's kitchen and made himself a plate of food, then sat back down on the barstool across from Leo.

"So, I heard that the B&B owner is coming into town next weekend." Leo smiled.

Jeremy shook his head. "Isabella Carter. Has she ever been able to keep a secret?"

"Well…" Leo swirled a piece of sirloin through the marsala sauce on his plate. "Now that you mention it, no. Isa can't keep a secret. So do you need a night off next weekend?"

"I was going to ask you if I could have next Sunday off. The wedding is Saturday, so Alison and Nicholas will be busy that day. They're staying at Ethan and Isa's house that night. But Sunday I was hoping to take them around for a fun day in Denver. They're coming into town Friday, but I'm going to stay on the schedule. Alison said that she and Nic want to have dinner at Romano's when I'm cooking."

Leo grinned. "Then you can really impress her. Tell her to order the sirloin marsala with mushrooms. You'll win her heart for sure."

Jeremy chuckled but the comment stuck with him later that night after his shift at the restaurant.

Win her heart? Then what?

Move to Estes Park? And do what? Work at one of the so-so restaurants I visited while I was there? Start my own restaurant in a tiny tourist town?

Despite the late hour, Jeremy went to the gym at the condo complex where he lived. He ran on the treadmill until his legs burned, then sat on a bench and downed a Gatorade, sweat dripping down his neck.

I love my job. Being a chef at Romano's is the perfect occupation for me. I get to create dishes like I did tonight for Leo. I get to run my own kitchen. I like the fast pace of the restaurant business.

His mind drifted to Alison. She'd mentioned having two weekends with visitors at the B&B, but he knew that wasn't enough to pull her out of her difficult financial situation. Not for the first time, Jeremy thought about the B&B and what role he might ever have a chance to play in its future.

The B&B had been Alison and Connor's livelihood. They had started it together, had run it together—it had been their dream. He had no idea whether she could ever share that dream with anyone else. And he didn't think she knew either. *She won't let go of the B&B, but I don't know if it's the business she won't let go of...or if it's Connor.*

He felt anxious to see her again. He knew his feelings for her hadn't waned, but what if hers had? He'd thought about Alison every day since he'd left Estes Park. But what if they saw each other again and the spark was gone?

For himself, Jeremy couldn't imagine that happening. Alison so consumed his thoughts—except for when he was working. He'd learned a long time ago to focus on cooking and to clear his mind of distractions when he was on the clock.

As he zipped up his duffel bag and prepared to head back up to his condo, he was surprised to see that he'd missed a call from his mom. A long voice mail from her brought a smile to his face. It had been several months since his last trip to Santa Fe to see her. From the message, it sounded as though his mom was as spry and cheerful as ever. She lived alone but was active in her community and had a group of women friends that she enjoyed spending time with. Jeremy was glad she sounded happy. He wondered about his sister, June. Two years younger than him and a full-time high-school English teacher, he knew her schedule was jam-packed. His mother had mentioned a few months ago that June was seriously dating someone, but Jeremy hadn't heard much more about it.

It's been too long since I've seen Mom and June. I need to make plans to head to New Mexico for Thanksgiving. Mom will be thrilled if I offer to cook Thanksgiving dinner.

He unlocked the door to his condo and walked in, tossing his keys on the table by the entryway and dropping his bag on the floor. The tall windows on the far side of his small condo gave him a great view of the city. He especially liked the view at night—when the lights made the city seem alive even after dark.

But as he stood in the kitchen and looked out at the bright city, his thoughts wandered back to Estes Park. He missed being so close to all that nature had to offer. He enjoyed hearing the soft crunch of the leaves when he walked down the path behind Alison's house. And he liked knowing the river was within reach. The Denver lights in front of him looked beautiful, but he missed the quiet stillness of the mountains at night, and rather than a host of flickering lights illuminating a city, he missed the moon shining like a spotlight over the mountains.

By Friday, Jeremy's nerves had him on edge. He stood over a hot stove as he simultaneously watched his marsala sauce simmer and checked the status of the minestrone soup. He looked at the clock, knowing that Alison and Nicholas had a seven o'clock reservation.

6:54. She's probably already here. Just a few steps away.

He wanted to go out to the dining room, but he couldn't leave a kitchen full of orders. He figured things would let up eventually and he'd go out to see Alison and Nic. Friday nights were crazy busy at Romano's and this evening was proving to be no exception. Jeremy was glad he'd made a reservation for Alison. He'd also let Angelina, the manager and Leo's cousin, know that he'd be picking up the tab for the Taylors' meal. Leo had let members of the staff know that Jeremy had a special guest coming in. Jeremy didn't mind; he wanted Alison to receive the VIP treatment.

The kitchen ran like a well-oiled machine with Jeremy in charge. The smell of garlic bread coming out of the oven swirled through the room, making Jeremy just a twinge hungry. Waiters rushed past him carrying plates of chicken parmesan, shrimp Alfredo, and Leo's famous lobster magnifico. Jeremy added salt to the soup, and then removed his marsala sauce from the heat.

"Table for two. One spaghetti and meatballs and one sirloin marsala," one of the waitresses, Jodi, called out as she walked into the room. Jeremy glanced up at Jodi and she winked at him.

Alison's here.

He looked back down and kept working, though he did take extra care to make sure Alison's order went out perfectly. Forty-five minutes had passed when he felt a tap on his shoulder.

Leo Romano stood next to him, an apron around his waist.

"All right, chef. I've got this covered. Go greet the guests, if you don't mind."

Jeremy wiped his brow and nodded. "I won't be long."

He washed his hands before leaving the kitchen, then made his way through the Romano's dining room. He paused at a table on his right, saying hello and asking how the food was. He did this twice more before heading to table 14. Alison saw him coming before he reached them. Jeremy could see Nic, as usual, talking a mile a minute. But Alison's gaze had shifted to him and they locked eyes.

Her blond hair looked soft and lovely, and her brown blouse matched the color of her eyes. A simple gold necklace rested on her neck.

As Jeremy reached the table, Nicholas jumped out of his seat.

"Jeremy!" Nic gave him a hug. But Alison didn't budge from where she sat.

"Can you join us, Chef?" she asked.

Jeremy sat in the chair next to her. They just looked at each other for a minute and Jeremy wondered if she felt it.

The spark between them.

To be fair, Jeremy thought it was more of an explosion than a spark.

"Did you make the spaghetti, Jeremy?" Nicholas asked.

Jeremy shook his head. "Sorry, pal. My sous chef, Margo, made the spaghetti tonight. How was it?"

"Good," Nicholas said with a shrug. Jeremy grinned.

"Did she make the sirloin marsala?" Alison asked. "It was so delicious. Really. It's my new favorite dish."

Satisfaction swept over Jeremy, but he maintained a collected composure.

"I made the sirloin marsala. I'm glad you liked it."

"I had a feeling you made it," Alison said with a smile and a tilt of her head as she looked over him.

"How did you know?" Jeremy asked. The buzz of the restaurant, even Nicholas's chatter, faded away as Jeremy watched Alison, waiting for her response.

She leaned closer to him. "Because it was perfect."

Chapter 17

Alison turned from side to side in front of the full-length mirror.

"I love that dress."

Alison swirled around to see Isabella in the doorway.

"Isabella!"

"You can call me Isa, Alison. And I really love that dress."

Alison turned back to the mirror. The straight, navy dress that reached just above her knees was one of her favorites. The wide neck and three-quarter-length sleeves always made her feel elegant, like she was Audrey Hepburn in one of those old black and white movies.

"I bought it years ago," Alison said, smoothing the fabric. "I haven't worn it in a long time." Seeing herself in it seemed strange.

Isabella moved to stand next to her. The two women were framed in the mirror. Isabella placed a comforting arm around Alison.

"I think today is the perfect day to wear it."

"A fall wedding. When we were in college, Nancy always talked about having a fall wedding."

"Are you sure you want to take Nicholas? I don't mind watching him," Isabella offered. "Layla and I are home today while Ethan runs the café."

"No, Nancy wants to see him. She hasn't seen him since he was in kindergarten."

"Gotcha. Well, I'm sure you'll have a wonderful time."

"By the way, I think I need your help redecorating my B&B. This guest room is impressive." Alison motioned to the room around them. From the drapes to the bedding to the comfy chair in a reading nook, the guest room was cozy and inviting.

"Oh, I can't take any credit. My idea of decorating begins and ends with a can of paint. My mother is a professional. She worked as an interior decorator for years. When we bought this house, her housewarming gift to me was a design plan. She took over," Isabella chuckled. "Now you should get going. Have fun, Alison."

Alison told her legs to move, but she stayed fixed in place. "I'm a little nervous," she admitted. "I've sort of… been avoiding things like this for a while."

Isabella nodded with empathy. "That's understandable, Alison," she said softly. "Just put one foot in front of the other. You're going to be okay."

An hour and a half later, Alison reminded herself of those very words as she took her seat beside Nicholas at the reception. She'd tried not to, but she'd cried at the wedding. Nancy looked so beautiful and seemed so happy that Alison hadn't been able to stop herself. She'd worked hard to keep memories of her own wedding day as far away as possible. If she started thinking about Connor, more tears would come and that wasn't how she wanted to spend her friend's happy day.

"Alison Clark?"

Alison looked up.

"Peter?"

Looking down at her was Peter Montgomery. They'd dated in college back when Alison roomed with Nancy. Alison's mouth opened and closed again. She couldn't quite find the words.

"Apparently, I'm assigned to this table." He pointed to the name card next to Nicholas.

"Did Nancy never mention that we were in medical school together?" he asked, obviously taking note of Alison's shocked face. He took his seat and leaned forward. Alison had to think.

"She might have," Alison admitted. Over the course of ten years since college, Alison would readily admit that knowing what had happened to Peter Montgomery hadn't been anywhere close to a priority or even an interest.

"I'm Alison Taylor now," she managed to say. "And this is my son, Nicholas."

Nicholas looked up from the handheld video game occupying his attention. "Hi," he mumbled.

"Hi yourself. Nice to meet you, Nicholas," Peter said kindly. Alison wondered if Nancy had ever mentioned to him that Connor had passed away. She hoped so. Alison didn't want to have to explain anything. By the way Peter never asked about her ringless finger or her absent husband, she came to the conclusion that Nancy must have told him. She also began to wonder if Nancy was trying to set them up by placing them at the same table.

A married couple joined their table, and dinner was served. Peter seemed so unlike the young man she'd known in college. He looked the same, except that his hairline was slightly more receding than she remembered. He'd been reserved and shy, obsessed with schoolwork. Now he seemed self-confident and assured, an oral surgeon with a well-established practice. Alison couldn't help wondering what he thought of her. Had she changed very much?

Of course I have. I've changed more than he could ever know. I went from being a carefree college girl to an in-love wife with a wonderful future to a single mom trying to keep up with her mortgage.

And then I met Jeremy.

Alison listened as Peter told her about his life—graduating from medical school, beginning his practice in Texas, almost getting married, then moving back to Denver. Nicholas went past wiggling to straight-out boredom, so Alison let him join some children playing in the reception hall.

The room was dimly lit and tables surrounded a dance floor filled with couples. Alison clapped as Nancy and her husband had their first dance, continued to talk with Peter as they ate wedding cake and didn't quite know what to do when Peter asked her to dance.

She was saved from making a decision when she saw Nancy wave at her from the bridal party table. Excusing herself, she rushed over, squealing with Nancy and wrapping her in a tight hug. The two friends chatted and Nancy introduced her to her husband, Blake.

"You saved me. Peter Montgomery just asked me to dance," Alison whispered. Nancy's eyes lit up.

"Seriously? Why aren't you dancing?"

"*Nancy.*" Alison groaned. "Did you intentionally place us at the same table?"

Nancy shrugged. "I made the seating chart forever ago. And he's not the same guy you knew in college, Ali. Blake and I know him well. He's a great guy. I think he's reached a point in his life where he's looking for the right woman."

She's not me.

"I'm…I'm sort of interested in someone else," Alison said, the words nearly getting stuck in her throat. Nancy looked surprised, then pleased. She squeezed Alison's hand.

"I'm so glad to hear that, Ali." The women talked for a few more minutes, but Alison knew Nancy had a host of guests to speak to so she made her way back to the table, happy to see Nicholas back in his chair, even if he *was* scarfing down a huge piece of the chocolate wedding cake.

"…I can fly-fish now. And we have a river right behind our house." Alison caught the tail end of Nicholas's monologue to Peter, obviously sharing every one of his life's details.

"You run a bed and breakfast?" Peter said as she sat down. Alison nodded.

"I do. The Mountain View Bed and Breakfast."

"That's fantastic, Ali! You know, I've been wanting to take a weekend and go up to the mountains. Are the leaves still changing colors, or have they all fallen?"

Alison swallowed, not wanting to be rude, but also not exactly wanting to extend an invitation for Peter to visit them in the small chance he was interested in her and not just the scenery.

"Well, there's some color left, but…"

"But a lot of the leaves have fallen," Nicholas answered for her. "Do you know what my costume is this year for our church fall festival? My mom made me a Batman costume. It's totally cool."

Alison felt a smile creep up on her face at Nicholas's animation. He could go from zero to ninety miles per hour in seconds. Once he got used to someone, Nicholas transformed from quiet to chatterbox. Alison looked at Nicholas's dark hair and bright smile as he talked continuously to Peter, who hadn't been able to get a word in for several minutes.

"Hey, have you ever been to the Denver Aquarium? My friend is taking us there tomorrow. I hope they have sharks. If I wasn't going to be Batman this year, I was going to be Captain America. Do you like comic books? Do you like fishing?" Nicholas's chatter didn't slow down.

The night was dark and brisk by the time Alison loaded a sleepy Nicholas into the SUV and drove back to Isabella and Ethan's house. Once Nicholas was snug and asleep on the air mattress in the guestroom, Alison stretched out under the warm comforter on the bed beside him and pondered the day's events.

Peter Montgomery. That was a blast from the past, for sure.

He'd asked for her phone number before they'd parted

ways, a clear indication that he wanted to reestablish a friendship with her. But she'd politely refused. If anything, friendly attention from Peter had confirmed one thing in Alison's heart. She only had eyes for a certain chef.

Chapter 18

Jeremy looked across the table at Alison and Nicholas, unable to keep the smile from his face. Something about being with the two of them felt spot-on right. Alison was telling Nicholas to eat his pancakes and stop scraping the whipped cream off the top. Nicholas was begging for more chocolate milk. Alison gave Jeremy an apologetic look.

"We had a late night at the wedding reception. I think that's contributing to our...issues this morning," she explained.

"Ali," Jeremy said calmly. "We're good. Hey, Nic! Are you excited to go to the aquarium?"

Nicholas nodded, his mouth stuffed with pancake. Jeremy chuckled. "You know, the sooner you finish your breakfast, the sooner we can get out of here and head downtown."

Nicholas plunged back into his pancakes and sausage. Jeremy had picked up Alison and Nicholas, and now they were at Ethan and Isabella's café for brunch. To be honest, he was as excited as Nicholas. Their day included the aquarium and then dinner at Jeremy's condo. As they waited for the credit card receipt, a swarm of firefighters came barreling through the doors of the Second Chance Café.

Jeremy had explained that Ethan actually worked for the fire department next door. Ethan had opened the café after being injured on the job and thus having to take some time off. The café was decorated in a fire station motif and filled with memorabilia, including a ladder hanging parallel to the ceiling. Judging by the tables filled with firefighters, the café was an obvious favorite of the guys stationed next door.

Once Jeremy signed his receipt, he and Alison and Nicholas piled into his truck and they headed to the aquarium. As they walked through the cavelike surroundings, marveling over the sea creatures, Jeremy leaned close and whispered to Alison, "Am I allowed to hold your hand?"

She smiled. "I think that's allowed."

Jeremy linked their hands. Nicholas did a double-take once he noticed, but after that he didn't seem bothered by the gesture. They turned a corner and Nicholas ran up to the glass. Alison dropped Jeremy's hand and put both hands on Nicholas's shoulders as they admired the eels swimming by.

"Alison! Hi, Nicholas!"

Jeremy turned to see who was speaking. Alison turned, too and looked stunned.

"Peter? What are you doing here?"

"Nic mentioned you two would be at the aquarium today. I didn't have anything going on, so I thought I'd try to meet up with you two and see if I could treat you to lunch."

Jeremy didn't move. *Who is this guy?*

Alison still looked shocked. Nicholas looked from his mother to Peter.

"This is our friend Jeremy," Nicholas said, pointing to Jeremy.

Thanks, buddy.

All right. Stay cool. This is not a big deal. I'm sure Ali has an explanation for how she knows this guy. Regardless, Nicholas is watching every move I make. I need to handle this well.

Jeremy swallowed any immediate feelings of jealousy— or at least masked them—and stepped forward, reaching out in an offer to shake Peter's hand.

"Jeremy Mitchell. Nice to meet you," he said, his voice

purposefully even. Peter glanced at Jeremy and shook his hand.

"Peter Montgomery. I didn't realize—" Peter looked back at Alison, then smoothly looked over at Jeremy again. "Ali and I go way back."

Ali?

"We went to college together," Alison broke in. "And Peter was at Nancy's wedding yesterday."

"Peter sat with us at the party," Nicholas piped up with his two cents. "He's never fly-fished, Jeremy," he added. Jeremy could have laughed at Nicholas's choice to share that detail with him in that awkward moment. He looked at Alison and wished he knew what she was thinking.

"Well, it was nice to see you, Peter." Alison said after a moment. "But we're here with Jeremy today and we better keep moving. We haven't seen the tigers yet."

Relief washed over Jeremy.

"Ali, could I talk to you for a minute?" Peter asked.

Short-lived relief.

"Um, well…" Alison's eyes darted to Jeremy.

"Go ahead," Jeremy said. "I've got Nic."

"Okay. I'll just be a sec." She and Peter stepped aside and Jeremy nudged Nic's shoulder.

"Come on, Nic. The tigers are around the corner."

They walked together slowly. "Tigers don't live underwater. I wonder why they're at the aquarium," Nic said.

"Good question," Jeremy said, his thoughts stuck on Alison and Peter. "Peter and your mom were friends when she was in college?" Jeremy said.

Nicholas shrugged. "I guess. He said he's been wanting to go up to the mountains."

"Really?" Jeremy's heart rate jumped.

"Hey, guys, I'm back," Alison rushed up to join then.

Nicholas grinned. "Mom, Jeremy and I want to know why there are tigers at the aquarium. They don't swim!"

Alison laughed. "Tigers can swim!"

All three of them laughed together and they continued through the maze of the aquarium. As they walked, Alison slid her hand back into Jeremy's. He looked down at her and raised an eyebrow.

"I'll explain later," she whispered.

Good enough for me.

Jeremy let go of the unease of the moment and concentrated on the day at hand.

Once they finished their tour of the aquarium, they had lunch at the restaurant, with Nicholas insisting on sitting right by the tank and squealing and giggling every time the big shark swam by.

After lunch, Jeremy took them to the Sixteenth Street Mall, a staple of downtown Denver and a great place to walk outside and enjoy the brisk autumn air. They stopped for ice cream and meandered through the outdoor mall, leaves swirling on the street around them and a street band's tunes filling their ears.

When the brisk air turned even colder, Jeremy suggested they head back to his condo. Walking down the street back to his truck, with Alison's small smooth hand tucked safely in his and Nicholas chomping on a waffle cone in front of them, Jeremy again felt that sense of family that had come over him during his stay at the B&B.

He tried not to let his thoughts drift to the inevitable reality that Alison and Nicholas would be leaving for Estes Park the following day. And even more disconcerting, Nicholas's revelation that Peter Montgomery wanted to take a trip to the mountains.

Back in his condo, Jeremy seasoned chicken pieces for baking while Alison peeled potatoes. Nicholas sat on the sofa, glued to the iPad in his hands.

"So, are you going to fill me in on your friend Peter and what that was all about?" Jeremy didn't want to push but was not willing to wait any longer before getting the story.

Alison dried her hands on a dishtowel. "We dated in college."

Jeremy blinked.

Okay. That was unexpected.

"Were you two…serious back then?"

Alison shook her head. "Oh, no. He was super shy and kind of a workaholic. But we did go out a few times. He knew my roommate, Nancy. After undergrad, he and Nancy went to medical school and I guess they kept in touch. So he was at the wedding and also at our table at the reception; I think that we were strategically placed near each other."

Perfect.

"And he showed up at the aquarium to see you," Jeremy surmised. Alison looked a little embarrassed.

"Yeah. Nicholas, of course, told him we were going to the aquarium today. But I had absolutely no idea he'd show up! I'm still shocked by that."

I'm not.

"I haven't seen him since college. Anyway, I think he was hoping we might be…friends again."

I'll bet he was.

From where he stood, Jeremy took in the picture that was Alison. Her blond hair was tied back in a sleek ponytail. She wore a long, creme-colored sweater over dark navy jeans and tall brown boots.

Jeremy had a feeling that grief and stress had so dominated Alison for the past couple of years that she probably had no idea how incredibly beautiful she was without even trying. And although in some ways she seemed frail—from her bereavement and the loss she'd sustained—she was unwaveringly strong, exuding confidence as a mother and her acceptance of herself and her situation.

Jeremy had never met anyone quite like her.

And he was pretty sure a special woman like Alison didn't just happen to stroll into his life by accident.

God, I believe you brought Alison into my life. I just need a little direction on how to keep her.

It occurred to Jeremy that he had no claim over Alison whatsoever. She was free to date whomever she wanted.

So was he, for that matter.

Except he wasn't.

"Ali," Jeremy said, lowering his voice so as not to draw Nicholas into the conversation.

She set aside one peeled potato and reached for another. "What?"

"You're really beautiful."

She paused, potato in hand. A smile spread across her face.

"Thanks, Jeremy. And you don't have anything to worry about, you know. I'm not interested in Peter. I told him that."

"He's interested in you."

Alison finished peeling the potato and rinsed it under the faucet. "Jeremy Mitchell, are you jealous?" she asked, her eyes amused.

He wanted to say no, but the truth was that the thought of Alison dating anyone other than himself—something he'd never even considered before Peter Montgomery showed up—made him extremely uncomfortable.

"Maybe a little," he confessed. She turned off the water. "But I can deal with it," he added quickly. "I know we haven't known each other for a very long time…and I live here and you're in Estes Park. We're dating but I don't have any expectations—I mean, I hope things will—I want us to—"

"Jeremy," Alison said softly. He stopped talking. "I'm only interested in you. And you're right—we haven't known each other very long. And we do have a bit of a geography problem. But I still like you."

"I like you too," Jeremy said with relief.

I really like you. More than I've ever liked anyone else.

In fact, I'm in love with you.

He held back the thought, knowing it wasn't the right time but also knowing it was true.

After dinner together, Jeremy took Alison and Nicholas back to Ethan and Isabella's home. After such a long day, Nicholas fell asleep almost instantly. Isabella poured cups of coffee and the four adults sat together in the living room.

"Have you told Alison you'll be running Romano's on Fifteenth for two weeks, Jeremy?" Isabella asked.

Alison looked at him with surprise. "Really? Where's Leo going?"

"My brother and his wife are going to Italy for two weeks," Isabella answered.

"They're taking the kids, right?" Jeremy questioned, referring to Leo and Mandy Romano's two children, Antonio and Olivia.

"Oh definitely. Olivia's only six months old. Mandy doesn't like to be more than five feet from her," Isabella joked. She turned to Alison. "My sister-in-law is a food critic, Alison. A really good one, I might add. Her endorsement of a place is pretty sought after. She also freelances for the TV show *Take Me There*. Sometimes they send her to do reviews on hotels and restaurants. A new resort opened in Rome and *Take Me There* wants Mandy to review it. She said she would as long as they didn't mind if her family went with her. So Leo's leaving Jeremy in charge."

"You'll do a great job," Alison said to Jeremy. He appreciated her faith in him.

"I hope so. Our manager, Angelina, will help a lot."

"Angelina just got engaged, Jeremy, so don't expect her to be overly concerned about the restaurant," Isabella said with a light laugh. The foursome stilled at the sound of whimpering coming from the baby monitor. Isabella jumped up and excused herself to check on the baby; Ethan followed her.

"So, you'll be running Romano's for two weeks?" Alison echoed.

Jeremy shrugged. "I run the kitchen most of the time anyway. But I'll tag team running the place with Angelina and make sure we're well staffed while Leo's gone."

They heard the baby crying through the monitor and Ethan and Isabella cooing and trying to soothe her.

"I remember when Nicholas was a baby. Connor and I were the same way. We'd jump if he made the slightest noise." Alison looked down at her cup of coffee. "They grow so fast. I can't believe Nic's already eight years old."

"Speaking of Nicholas, he seemed okay with us holding hands today," Jeremy commented.

"I told him we're dating. He likes you, Jeremy. Believe me, he'd tell me if he didn't. When I mentioned to him that I like you a lot, Nic's response was, 'Well, at least he can fix things.'"

Jeremy laughed. "It's lucky I can fix a leaky faucet, I guess."

Alison smiled back and Jeremy took the moment to lean over and give her a quick kiss.

"Lucky for both of us," she agreed. Alison shifted uneasily in her seat and Jeremy worried for a moment that the kiss had been a bad idea.

"As much as I like you, though, Jeremy, I need to tell you that I have to take things very slowly."

Jeremy sat back and nodded. "I know. I'm sorry."

Alison shook her head. "You don't have to apologize. The truth is that I want you to kiss me," she said, with a trace of guilt lacing her words. "But I have to think about the future. I worry things won't work out and Nicholas and I will be disappointed. I worry things *will* work out and that I'm bringing more change into Nicholas's life when he's had about as much as he can take. I'm worried about losing the business. I set Christmas as my deadline to decide whether to sell or not. Other than those two weekends, I haven't had any other bookings. What if Christmas comes and goes and then I have to tell Nicholas we're moving?"

"Things may pick up yet, Ali. You're about to be featured in several publications. It could generate bookings and revenue." Jeremy hoped to encourage her.

"I know. And I'm hopeful. But I'm also coming to the conclusion that I have to give the business to God. I have to have faith that even if I can't keep it, He's got a plan for me and Nic. You'd think I'd have learned that lesson by now…" Alison's voice caught and she took in a shaky, shallow breath. "The lesson of not holding on so tightly to things. The lesson that anything—even something precious—can slip through our fingers."

Jeremy felt emotion flood his heart. He reached over and took Ali's cold hand in his.

"He didn't slip through your fingers, Ali," Jeremy said. "He's with God. You'll see Connor again."

With effort, Alison looked at him. "I'm afraid of more losses."

Jeremy squeezed her hand. "I know."

"I'm afraid of change, too," she said in a thin voice. Jeremy was certain she was holding back tears. "But I'm working on giving that to God. It seems to be something He keeps bringing into my life."

Jeremy took that moment to ask the question that he'd been thinking for weeks.

"Do you think—I just wondered if you could ever see yourself living somewhere other than Estes Park. I know how much you love it up there." Jeremy could hear the hope in his own words.

He watched Alison struggle to swallow before speaking. "I don't know. That would be an extreme change for me. I'll be honest and tell you that that's not something I want to happen. But I guess…if God wants to move me somewhere…maybe I would," she said honestly.

Jeremy nodded.

It's something.

"Jeremy, right now, my priority is maintaining a home for Nicholas. He needs stability, and I have to provide that for him. A relationship with you has to come second to that. And I don't know if I'm going to turn things around for the B&B by Christmas, but I know I'm going to try."

Jeremy looked at their entwined hands. "You don't have to do everything alone, Ali," he said tenderly. Jeremy hoped she took every one of his words to heart. "I can help."

Chapter 19

Alison skimmed her grocery list, taking a look at the packed cart in front of her. "Is Jeremy coming for Thanksgiving?" her mother asked. Alison shook her head and maneuvered the cart to the checkout lane.

"He's going to New Mexico to see his mom and his sister. His sister is dating someone and Jeremy hasn't met him yet."

Her mother moved in front of her and started emptying the cart items onto the counter.

"And Michelle is going to see her parents?" her mom asked.

"Right. As long as the weather cooperates. If we have snow, she'll probably stay in town and join us. Is there anyone else you want to invite? Some church friends who need a place to go?" Alison wondered. For all of her life, Alison's family had rarely celebrated a holiday when her mother hadn't found a few stragglers to bring into the family fold. It was a character trait that Alison hoped to emulate.

"I wouldn't rule out the possibility," her mother said.

"I'll miss Jeremy at Thanksgiving. I was hoping he'd spend the holiday with us," Alison acknowledged. Her mother nodded.

"I'm sure he'll make it out here sometime during the holiday season. We'll have a wonderful Thanksgiving together, dear. Don't worry. Your father's looking forward to a whole day with Nicholas. Have you had any reservations at the B&B since the ads came out?"

"Well, a few promotional ads don't run until December. But I have gotten some feedback from the ones that went out this month. I booked a few weekends in January. But I'm staying with my Christmas deadline. We'll host people in January, of course, but unless December is a spectacular month, I'm going to talk to a realtor in January."

Her mother looked pained. "I know that's a hard decision for you, Alison. But I think you're doing the right thing. You can't keep going on like this."

"I know," Alison sighed, the burden of her decision hovering over her like a black storm cloud. Her mother started going over their Thanksgiving menu and Alison listened only halfheartedly. The holiday didn't carry with it the excitement it normally did. At least, the excitement it had before she lost Connor. Before she felt overwhelmed by her financial situation. Before her life had turned upside down.

On Wednesday, Alison cooked cornbread and chopped vegetables to prep for Thanksgiving dinner. Alone with her thoughts, she worried that she still didn't have a single reservation for December. A knock at the door startled her. She opened the door to find Michelle on her doorstep.

"Shawn just left with Darius," Michelle said, her eyes wet. Alison opened the door wide.

"Come in," she said. Michelle walked in and Alison pulled her into a tight squeeze.

"You're not alone. You're not alone," she whispered. Michelle nodded, obviously on the verge of crying again.

"I feel alone," Michelle said.

"I know." Alison held her tighter. "But you're not. I'm glad you're here." Alison leaned back and held her at arm's length. "Come in and help me cook, Michelle. Nic's spending the night at Mom and Dad's."

"You might as well give me the onions to chop," Michelle said and Alison chuckled.

"You're not leaving town, right? Not with all the snow predicted for tomorrow?" Alison clarified.

"No. I don't want to chance driving through the mountains in bad weather. I figure I'll eat here and spend the day after Thanksgiving watching old movies and eating pecan pie."

"Excellent plan. Except you should come over and we'll watch movies together. Holiday movie marathon."

The kitchen warmed as Alison and Michelle cooked. Michelle ended up rolling out dough for two pies. Once the dishwasher was whirring and the house smelled like pecan pie and cornbread, the two friends sat on Alison's sofa, arms linked.

"Michelle," Alison said. "How did you get through it? How did you get past Darius leaving and your family breaking up?"

Michelle sighed. "I learned what you've learned, Ali." Michelle's gaze drifted off. "That hard and aching and beautiful truth—that when someone you love is gone," Michelle's voice shook, "you wake up and Jesus is still there."

Alison began crying without warning at the undeniable verity of that statement. She and Michelle gripped hands, comforting each other with the love of a friendship that ran deep.

"You're right," Alison said through her tears. "That's how we get through it. That's how we keep getting through it. I've been thinking of that scripture that says God is my strength and my song. But so many days I feel shattered and alone. Like I have no strength left."

"Me too," Michelle said, wiping her eyes. "But He *is* our strength, Ali. And our song."

"And we have each other," Alison added, desperately thankful for the friend next to her who understood those broken moments.

"Every step of the way," Michelle assured her. After a quiet moment, Michelle reached for a tissue from the box on the end table and wiped her nose. "How are things going with Jeremy?"

Alison laid her head back on the sofa. "I miss him. I think. Maybe I just miss Connor. Maybe the loneliness isn't really about Jeremy being in Denver. It all goes back to Connor."

"I don't believe that, Alison. Do you? Really?"

"I'm not sure," Alison admitted. "Connor was the love of my life. I'm not romanticizing our marriage. It wasn't perfect. We had ups and downs like everyone. But we loved each other so much. We were *so* happy. How could I ever find that kind of relationship again? He's *not* replaceable."

"Oh, Ali," Michelle said. "Of course he's not. Moving forward with your life in no way means replacing Connor. It's not about that. But you need to decide for yourself how you feel about Jeremy. From where I'm sitting, I think you're falling for the guy. Actually, I think you're past the point of falling for the guy."

"His chicken vesuvio is amazing." Alison sighed. Michelle snorted, resulting in giggles from both women.

Michelle headed home before the snow hit and Alison spent the next hour online, searching for rental houses and writing down the numbers of potential real-estate agents. The next day she ate turkey and green bean casserole and rolls with a host of people at her table. Michelle had come over first thing that morning and Alison's mother had, as usual, found new friends to include. A young family new to Estes Park and states away from their extended family and an elderly single man from their church congregation joined them for an early Thanksgiving dinner. By late afternoon, Alison stood at the back door, looking out over the snow-covered deck, feeling chilly and missing Jeremy.

I'm just lonely.

Is it really Jeremy I miss? Or is it Connor? Michelle's right. I need to figure that out, and soon.

Alison's heart argued with her mind. She didn't want to let Jeremy consume her thoughts. She didn't want to think about him so much. Not when she had a business to run and a son to raise. She kept thinking about their conversation at Ethan and Isabella's house, about whether Alison would ever be willing to move.

She couldn't even entertain the thought without feeling anxiety…and sadness.

She connected with the mountains and the river; small-town life suited her. The thought of taking Nicholas far from his grandparents stirred almost immediate tears from her. Leaving the B&B was one thing—one thing she could barely accept might happen soon.

But leaving Estes Park?

Father, I don't know what you want me to do. I like Jeremy. A lot. I might even love him, which, two years ago I would have thought to be impossible. But if being with him means giving up my home here—I don't know if I can do it.

Jeremy's special, there's no doubt about that. I never thought I would feel this way about someone again. I keep fighting against these feelings, but I'm not sure I want to.

Alison's phone buzzed on the kitchen counter and her heart leapt at the incoming text from Jeremy.

I guess I'm not doing a very good job of fighting my conflicted feelings.

She read the message.

Missing you guys this Thanksgiving. I'm sorry I can't be with you. Any chance I could come up next weekend?

Alison only hesitated for a moment.

Yes.

Jeremy smiled at Alison's immediate response. He felt certain Leo would give him the time off to return to Estes Park. Running Romano's while Leo and Mandy were in Italy had gone off without a hitch, but the sous chef had come down with pneumonia afterward, and so, with the exception of his trip to Santa Fe, Jeremy had been working on overdrive for nearly a month. He desperately needed a break.

He thought about Alison.

Father, my soul is thirsting for a river again. One right by Alison Taylor.

The prayer was one of many that had filled his heart since he'd last seen Alison and Nicholas. And now, spending Thanksgiving with his mother and June and Dylan—June's boyfriend whom Jeremy believed would soon be June's husband judging by the way his sister had stars in her eyes every time she looked in Dylan's direction—made Jeremy all the more lonely for Alison and Nicholas. He looked around the table, picturing them there with him, picturing them as part of his family.

He'd spoken to Alison briefly that morning and noticed the weariness in her voice when she mentioned that she still didn't have any guests lined up for December. Another month without income for her. And with it the festivities and expenses of Christmas.

He hoped the holiday didn't burden her with more stress.

I bring you good tidings of great joy that shall be unto all people.

The verse came quickly—a reminder.

Thank you for prompting that in my heart, Father. Christmas isn't an encumbrance. It's a gift. And I want it to be a source of joy for Alison this year. She's had enough grief and worry. It's time for joy.

Jeremy's mother served slices of pumpkin pie with homemade whipped cream and coffee. Jeremy listened to the conversation around the table, wondering how he could help make Alison's holiday a memorable one.

"Thanks, Mom," Jeremy said as he took a bite of his mother's made-from-scratch pie. She grinned at him.

"It's the least I could do after my handsome chef son cooked us a gourmet Thanksgiving meal. It is the season of giving, you know."

Season of giving.

Suddenly, Jeremy absolutely knew what would make all the difference for Alison Taylor this Christmas.

"Penny for your thoughts, son." His mother sat down next to him, stirred her coffee and waited. June and Dylan were deep in conversation, so Jeremy felt free to confide in his mother.

"I think I'm in love. Actually, I know I am."

His mother's jaw dropped, but she quickly recovered. "I see. Let me guess—the single mom you've mentioned several times."

Jeremy gave her a sheepish look. "Obvious?"

His mother shrugged. "If you love someone, hiding it is hard. And that's perfectly acceptable."

"But it could change everything."

His mother nodded, glancing over at June and Dylan. "True. But sometimes everything needs to change. And once it does, you realize God knew what He was doing all along. You realize that nothing is beyond Him."

Jeremy digested that thought, accepting it, holding on to it, feeling the truth of it sink into his mind.

"She's been through a lot. I told you…she lost her husband. I don't know if she's ready to let go of what her life with him looked like and start a new life with someone else."

"Well, then you meet her halfway. More than halfway. If you love her, you pursue her like God pursues us—relentlessly, passionately. Do you think you can do that?"

"I know I can," Jeremy said with conviction.

"I had a feeling that was the case," his mother said with a smile. "My son has always liked a challenge. I think I need to meet this woman, Jeremy."

"I'm sure she'd love to meet you. I'll make it happen as soon as I can," he promised. "I've been trying to come up with a special gift to give her for Christmas. A grand gesture of sorts. I think I've finally come up with an idea. I've figured out what she'd want most."

Jeremy's mom patted his hand. "And what do you want most this Christmas, son?"

Alison.

Nicholas.

From where he sat at the dining room table, Jeremy could see snow steadily beginning to fall outside.

"Family," he answered.

"Then that's my Christmas wish for you," his mother said firmly. "A family of your own."

Chapter 20

"The day after Christmas? Yes, we'll be open. One room for two. Got it. Two nights? Sure. We'll be glad to have you." Eight days after Thanksgiving, Alison took down the customer's credit card information over the phone and penciled the reservation into her calendar. She hung up her cell phone, thankful for the booking but hoping Nicholas wouldn't mind having company the day after Christmas. It couldn't be helped. They needed the money. At least they'd have Christmas together just as a family.

Christmas.

I still need to go shopping for Nicholas. He wants a fly rod, of course. I was hoping for a less expensive gift.

But I so want him to have a good Christmas. He's had a rough two years. Last Christmas was awful; I could barely bring myself to put up a tree. This Christmas I want Nicholas to know that we're going to be okay.

Alison finished entering all the booking information into her computer and, as usual, pulled up her bank account information to pay her bills and subsequently feel discouraged.

An hour later, she pushed away from her computer and glanced at the clock. Nicholas came up the stairs.

"Mom, have you looked outside? It started snowing again. I wish it would stop! I wanted to ride my bike."

"Well, it's cold today. But it's supposed to warm up somewhat next week. Forties at least. Which means if you bundle up, you'll be able to play outside. So just look forward to that."

"Are you sure Jeremy's coming today? Even if it snows?"

"That's what he said, kiddo. I'm sure he'll call if he has to turn back. We're not supposed to get much snow, so I think he'll make it."

"How long is he staying?"

Alison watched as Nicholas planted himself by the front window, preparing to wait for Jeremy. Her heart pulled at the sight.

"He didn't say. Probably just the weekend. I'm going to start working on dinner. Tell me when Jeremy drives up." About thirty minutes later, Alison heard Nicholas whoop and call out that Jeremy had arrived. She just smiled and let Nicholas let Jeremy in. She could hear them talking in the foyer before they walked into the kitchen. She looked up from where she stood at the stove and grinned at Jeremy.

"Hey, you," he said. Alison's heart rate picked up speed at the sight of the tall, blond, strikingly handsome chef who walked toward her and enveloped her in a hug.

"Hi," she said, smiling. "Hungry?"

"Definitely. What are we having?"

"Chicken curry with rice and veggies."

"Sounds great. Let me get settled upstairs and I'll come help."

She watched Jeremy leave the kitchen with Nicholas trailing after him.

The house feels fuller with him here.

She already dreaded him leaving.

After dinner Jeremy set his boots in the closet in the Dove room and unpacked his suitcase. Then he stretched out on the bed and closed his eyes. Slowly, he began to unwind. He'd wanted to be back at the B&B for weeks. He'd wanted to be with Alison and Nicholas. And now, here he was. After a hot, home-cooked meal with Ali and Nic,

Jeremy had helped clean up the kitchen and then finally retired to his room, tired from the drive earlier, which had included navigating through snow.

He hadn't shared his secret yet, his Christmas present for Alison. He hoped she'd be excited when he shared it with her.

Jeremy rolled off the bed, walked to the balcony and looked out at the night before him. The moon illuminated the river in the distance and light snow drifted down.

His relief at being back astounded him.

I knew I missed the river. I knew I missed Ali and Nicholas. But being here...I feel like I can finally breathe easy.
Like I'm home.

He hoped the snow would continue to be light. He needed a few clear, warm days to get everything done.

The next morning, Jeremy woke early, dressed warmly and made his way outside to chop firewood for Alison. Every moment by the river invigorated him. The time outdoors in the cold weather rejuvenated him. Afterward, he stomped the slight snow from his boots and marched into the house, pulling off his gloves and taking the cup of coffee Alison handed him.

"Where's Nic?" Jeremy asked, sitting down on one of the bar stools.

"Still asleep. I guess the excitement of having you back wore him out." Alison sat next to him and crossed her legs. An oversized Denver University sweatshirt hung down over her black stretch pants. Beneath, he could see pink polka dot socks on her feet. He looked at her over the top of his coffee cup.

"I really missed you," he told her. She looked down, obviously trying to hold back her smile.

"We missed you," she responded.

"Ali," Jeremy began. "You know I'm..." he stopped, not sure how to finish.

In love with you? Certain we're meant to be together?

He cleared his throat. "I've been trying to think of what to give you for Christmas. I finally came up with an idea—and I hope you'll accept it."

"What is it?" she asked warily.

"I've got some friends arriving the day after tomorrow. In fact, we might have company off and on all week."

"What do you mean?" Alison asked in disbelief. Jeremy set aside his coffee mug and put his hands on her shoulders.

"I want to help with a few of those house projects you need completed," he told her softly. "And I need you to *let me help you.*"

He could see her wrestle with her thoughts. He wasn't sure which side was winning, but after a moment, she seemed to fortify herself. "What's your plan?"

"We're going to do some outside repairs. I know the front porch needs a little work. We won't be able to paint the whole exterior until it's warmer, but I think we can do some touch-up painting this week. I noticed the extra cans of paint in your garage."

"What else?" she asked, her voice nervous.

"Whatever you need me to do. I have friends coming to help. Isabella mentioned you wanted to do some redecorating. Well, I have a friend who's going to be your consultant on that. She'll be here Monday, and I have a feeling she'll have some great ideas. My buddies and I can paint inside if you need us to. I can show you how to make a few new breakfast dishes, if you want me to. I also think we could update your website this week. We have a lot to do before Christmas. Are you okay with a few overnight guests? In some cases, I might have a friend or two drive up for the day. But if the weather's bad, I want them to know they have a place to sleep."

"Of course. That's not a problem. I should tell you that I just got a reservation for the day after Christmas. I keep hoping that because more ads are running this month, the calls will start coming in, but that's all I've got so far."

"I have faith that the B&B still has a bright future, Alison. You don't have guests right now, so let's use the opportunity to dress this place up and make it perfect for a holiday vacation."

She closed her eyes and he wondered if she was praying.

"Ali?" he said after a moment. She opened her eyes.

"Jeremy...I can't believe you're doing this for me. How will I ever pay you back? And I know you have to get back to work. How do you have time for all of this?"

Jeremy stepped close and cupped her face in his hands. "There is no paying me back, Ali. I *want* to do this. And I think God wants me to do this. So let me. Please. As for my job, I'm here for a week, longer if I need to be. And I have time for it because I'm making time for it. You're important to me. Saving this business is your priority, so that makes it my priority."

"It's too much, Jeremy. I can't let you do this."

"The Mountain View B&B is a special place. It deserves to be saved."

"And you think it can be? You think all these changes will be enough?" Alison crossed her arms and looked skeptical.

Jeremy nodded. "I think they're a really good start. And once we get through the makeover part of this endeavor, I have another surprise that might make all the difference."

Alison looked confused. "What else could there be?"

Jeremy kissed Alison—a deep, meaningful kiss that could leave no questions regarding how strong his feelings were for her. She opened her eyes afterward and just stared at him. He smiled.

"A Christmas surprise. Just leave it at that, Ali. We've got a busy week in front of us."

"Where do we start?"

"Well, by Monday one of my buddies will be here. He and I will start tackling the outside repairs, and Jennifer, your new best friend and a really great interior designer, is going to help you spruce up the inside of the B&B. If you're okay with it, Jen will drive up Sunday night so she can work with you all day Monday. She's already scoped out the pictures from the website and I know she'll have ideas. Jen's actually another one of Leo's cousins. I think Isa told you that Leo's mother worked for years as an interior decorator. She trained Jennifer, and now Jennifer helps with the restaurant decor and does some freelance design, too.

"Tuesday, another friend is coming up to help me finish the outside work and any inside work you need me to do. Wednesday morning, a friend is going to give you a crash course in updating your website over the phone. I wish I could help you with that, but I'm pretty tech challenged. But Eddie—he's done all the work on our Romano's websites—will walk you through some simple updates that should make the site more user-friendly."

Alison looked speechless.

Jeremy had a feeling it was time to slow down. She looked overwhelmed. Unable to resist, he tucked a stray blond strand behind her left ear and touched the braid that fell over her shoulder. "But, personally," he said, "I'd like to start with cutting down a Christmas tree. How does that sound?"

Alison's eyes lit up.

"I should warn you, I'm not a Charlie Brown Christmas tree kind of girl."

An immediate smile filled Jeremy's face. "Go big or go home?" She nodded and they both stood.

"Are you up for this?" she asked with an adorable grin that made Jeremy want to pick her up and swing her around. He stood still, though. Losing his composure wasn't his style. Jeremy just shrugged.

"Don't you know by now, Ali Taylor? I'm always up for a challenge."

Chapter 21

Sunday morning Alison walked into River Community Church with Jeremy Mitchell, and again, heads turned. They sat near the front, along with Nicholas and her parents, who seemed pleased to see Jeremy. After church, Alison's friends beelined over to their pew and took turns saying hello to Jeremy and questioning him about his latest visit. Alison heard him explaining to Mary Margaret that he and a few friends were helping with several house projects this week.

Alison finally managed to pry him from Mary Margaret's grip, and with hellos and goodbyes said to Michelle, Lenora, Cori and a slew of others, she, Jeremy and Nicholas filed out of the church. Jeremy hugged her mother and shook her father's hand before the three of them headed back to the B&B. Jennifer would be arriving that evening and there was much to do.

Alison and Jeremy spent the afternoon and early part of the evening walking around the perimeter of the house, talking through things that needed to be fixed. Jennifer arrived just in time for dinner. The two women walked through every room in the house while Jennifer talked paint colors and inexpensive redecorating tips with Alison. It was decided that they would go to the hardware store first thing in the morning and buy paint for almost the entire main floor of the house.

Jennifer had Jeremy carry in two large boxes of decorative items.

"They're from Rosalinda, Leo's mother and my aunt," Jennifer explained. "She's trying to purge her basement and told me to take whatever I deemed useful. So I basically grabbed everything I could carry, starting with this," Jennifer pulled a large white wreath from the top of the box.

"Oh, it's beautiful!" Alison exclaimed. Jennifer nodded in agreement.

"It's time for a little holiday spirit, Alison," she said. Alison's throat constricted. She watched as Jennifer hung the wreath on the front door, amazed by how something so small could mean so much.

It's just a wreath. Get hold of yourself.

Alison felt like she'd fallen into a well of emotion and every little thing caused the well to stir and rise, turning her into a weepy mess.

But with her extensive experience with grief, this felt different. When Connor died, Alison had cried what seemed like every hour for weeks, unable to ever reach a point where she didn't feel as though she were drowning. The time between the tears eventually increased—but the tears felt the same. Hopeless. Devastated. Distraught.

Father, this feels like a new kind of brokenness. It doesn't quite make sense to me. But I almost feel like this hurt...is actually restoring me somehow. It's like I'm overwhelmed by hope this time. Rather than hopelessness.

Alison inhaled and repressed that rising well of emotion, not wanting to make Jennifer uncomfortable.

They all went to bed early, with Jeremy reminding them that they had a full day ahead of them. Alison tucked Nicholas in bed, listening as he said his bedtime prayers. Her heart ached just a little when he thanked God for sending Jeremy to their house.

Yes, Father. Her heart reverberated. *Thank you.*

She turned the lights off, but before she closed Nicholas's door, he called out to her, "Mom, are you happy about Christmas this year?"

Without turning the light back on, Alison sat back down on the bed by Nicholas.

"Of course I am."

"Last year it was kind of a sad Christmas," he said in a small voice. Alison nodded, even in the dark.

"I know, son."

"Do you still miss Dad?" he asked, his voice even smaller.

"Yes, I do," Alison assured him.

"Me, too. But I like it when Jeremy's here. Is that okay?"

Alison ran her fingers through Nicholas's hair and smoothed his blanket.

"Yes, it's okay. We'll always miss your dad. But Jeremy's our friend. I like it when he's here, too."

"Do you miss him when he goes to Denver?"

"I do."

"So do I. I'm happy about Christmas, Mom. And I've been thinking—you don't have to buy me a fly rod."

The emotional well filled right back up.

Oh, Lord. Thank you for this boy You gave me.

"We'll see, okay? Fly rod or not, this is going to be a great Christmas."

"Last year we only had that small plastic tree you put in the living room."

Alison's breath caught. She rubbed Nicholas's arm.

"I know, sweetie. Last year was really hard. But we made it through. And this year, we have the biggest tree I've ever seen."

Nicholas giggled. "It's huge!"

Alison chuckled. "I know! Did you see Jeremy's face when I picked that one out?"

Nicholas put a straight face on, copying Jeremy, and folded his arms. "You're sure, Ali?" He said in a deep voice, imitating Jeremy's reaction. That sent them both into another set of giggles. Alison leaned down and hugged him tightly, and this time Nicholas said good-night and rolled over to fall asleep without another word.

The next morning, Alison woke extra early, wanting to be as proactive as possible. She brewed a pot of coffee and put together some easy breakfast sandwiches for her guests before driving Nicholas to school. By the time she returned, Jennifer was dressed and waiting for her. They drove to the hardware store for gallons of a pale shade of grey paint. Jennifer assured her that it would brighten the downstairs and make it feel not only open but also larger.

Once they arrived home, another truck was parked in the driveway and Alison figured that Jeremy's friend had arrived. After quick introductions, Jeremy and Wes got to work outside. Alison and Jennifer moved furniture and prepared to paint. She'd just thrown a sheet over her sofa when the doorbell rang. Confused by why Jeremy wouldn't just walk in, Alison rushed to open the door.

There stood Mary Margaret, Michelle, Lenora and Cori.

"What in the world?" Alison said with surprise.

"Alison, why didn't you ask us for help?" Mary Margaret asked sternly. "I hope you have enough paintbrushes for all of us."

"If not, I brought more," Lenora said with a smile, holding up a plastic bag. The well rose back up in Alison as the four women bombarded her home.

"Remember, we're in this together. Every step of the way," Michelle whispered in her ear. Alison nodded but could barely speak.

"More recruits! Excellent!" Jennifer exclaimed. "Come on, ladies. Let's get started. This will go much faster with so many of us."

"We're family," Mary Margaret said to Alison. Mary Margaret still had the look of consternation plastered on her face.

"Speaking of family," Michelle said. "Alison, look."

Alison followed Michelle's gaze to the front window. She walked back to the front door and opened it just as her dad's pickup pulled into the circular drive. The well spilled over this time as her dad climbed from the truck. She rushed down the steps to greet him.

"Dad, what are you doing here?"

He kissed the side of her head. "Ali, I'm here to help, of course. Didn't Jeremy tell you I was coming?"

She shook her head and wiped her eyes. "I think he's on the roof actually."

Alison thought of her dad's wish for her to sell the place and move back home. That hadn't stopped him from showing up to support her desire to keep the B&B. As always, he was here when she needed him.

A memory flashed through her mind—the moment the doctor told Alison that Connor was gone. She'd stood in the hospital room with her parents and Connor's parents, who'd driven down from their home in Wyoming. The waiting room had been filled to capacity with friends and family members. But at that terrible moment, with her husband out of her reach forever, Alison's legs had given way beneath her as she'd cried out in total desperation. It had been her dad's strong arms that had held her up when she had no strength at all.

"I'd better find Jeremy and see where he needs me," her dad said, looking up toward the roof. But Alison just threw her arms around her father.

"I love you, Dad," she managed to say.

"I love you, too," he whispered back. "It's okay, Ali. It will all be okay."

She looked up at the sound of another SUV pulling into the now-crowded driveway. Mary Margaret's husband, Paul; Cori's husband, Dwayne; and Pastor Daniel from River Community climbed out.

"We're here to help, Ali. Tell us what you need," Pastor Daniel called out. Alison buried her head in her dad's chest and wept. Holding back her tears wasn't possible.

"Come on now, honey," her father said quietly, lifting Alison's chin. He smiled at her but Alison saw tears in his eyes, too. "This is what we do. We show up for each other." He headed toward the house. "Your mother said not to worry about lunch. She's bringing sandwiches at noon and she's been baking cookies all morning."

Alison felt someone touch her back and she turned to see Mary Margaret. "Dry those eyes. There's a wall in the living room with your name on it, Alison. Let's go paint." Mary Margaret put an arm around Alison and they walked back into the house together. The gentle pressure of her friend's arm around her instilled a sense of comfort in Alison and helped her collect her emotions.

"I can't believe you all showed up to help. I didn't even ask."

Mary Margaret tsk-tsked. "And you should have, Alison. Every person here cares about you. We want to help you make this business succeed. But don't forget that this was all orchestrated by Jeremy. The fact that that man is up on your roof, patching shingles in December, tells me that his love language is service. And he's serving you, Alison."

Alison's heart pounded.

"Hey, Ali!" She jumped off the porch, shielded her eyes and looked up. Jeremy stood on the roof, a tool belt around his waist.

"Could you bring out some water bottles?"

She just looked at him for a moment, then nodded. "Water bottles. Right. Sure," she stammered, her thoughts all over the place. She numbly walked into the kitchen, passing the living room where her friends were already painting, the sounds of their conversation and laughter drifting through the house. But Alison barely heard them. Her thoughts were glued to Mary Margaret's observant comments about Jeremy's love language being service and how he was serving Alison—in huge ways.

He loves me.

He's done all this because he loves me.

This will change everything.

Alison stood alone in the kitchen, holding on to the counter to keep her steady.

Father, show me what to do.

Chapter 22

Jeremy rolled his neck, fatigue taking over. The sun was sinking behind the snow-capped mountains. It was time to call it a day. Wes packed up his tools and Jeremy invited him to join them for dinner before leaving for Denver. They'd been friends since Jeremy's first time visiting their church in Denver and had much in common, including their experience in construction.

Jeremy knew that friends from Ali's church had brought over casseroles for the evening meal. Michelle had left earlier to pick up Nicholas and Shawn, and the boys had run around like combustible balls of energy until Ali's dad gave them the task of cleaning up the garage. Ali's community of family and friends impressed Jeremy. It was the kind of community he'd always longed for—a network of believers who lived life together in tangible ways.

He wiped his boots on the rug out front before walking through the front door. He froze.

"What do you think?" Alison asked, walking down the hallway toward him with a big smile on her face.

"Am I in the same house?"

"No kidding. Jennifer is incredible. I don't know what she did, but somehow this looks like a new house."

Jeremy took in his surroundings. The new, pale grey color on the walls opened up the house substantially. Jennifer had rearranged nearly all the furniture in the living and dining areas, and she'd placed new accent pillows on the sofas and chairs. Somehow, those minor changes created an entirely new feel throughout the house. A few new pieces of colorful art, strategically placed to quickly draw the eye, created splashes of just the right amount of color on the muted walls. New vases held tall white branches as centerpieces for the dining room. From the branches hung small white Christmas ornament balls. Jeremy noticed that the formerly brown coffee table had been stripped and painted a bright teal.

And standing regally near the front bay window of the living room, Alison's massive Christmas tree twinkled. Jennifer had decorated the tree to perfection. Lights on the tree, garland on the staircase, multiple candles of different shapes and sizes on the mantle, a nativity scene on the antique buffet table—the subtle but classic decorations infused holiday spirit into the house.

"It looks—" Jeremy began.

"Beautiful." Alison finished. "I love it. I was never crazy about that whole quaint, rustic B&B design. Connor and I had always hoped to update the decor and make our B&B a little different from the others around here. This is the perfect start. Thank you, Jeremy, for asking Jennifer to come."

Alison ran her finger along his jawline, then raised up on her tiptoes and kissed him.

Jeremy didn't move.

That's the first time she's initiated a kiss between us. Something's changed.

She stepped back, a contented smile on her face. Jeremy took her hand in his. "Well, we replaced some shingles. Touched up paint in lots of areas. Replaced and painted the steps on the front porch and replaced a few boards on the deck. Your dad installed a new railing on the right side of the deck. And come see." He pulled her with him to the front porch and closed the front door.

Alison squealed. "You painted my front door! Oh wow!" The front door was now completely black, with the large, stark-white wreath hanging front and center. White faux poinsettia plants stood on either side of the door against the grey house.

"Michelle brought the poinsettias," he told her.

"It's just…stunning, Jeremy," she said.

"I can't take the credit. It was Jennifer's idea. I just painted the door," he said with a shrug.

The door opened and Jolene poked her head out. "Come in, you two. It's getting cold out here and we've got a smorgasbord of food."

Alison and Jeremy exchanged an amused glance. "Okay, Mom. We're coming." Hands intertwined, they joined the crowd of people milling about and eating in the kitchen.

By the time the guests had all left and Nicholas was sound asleep, Jeremy fell into his bed upstairs, knowing full well every muscle would be aching the next morning… and not caring one bit.

The light, the hope—and what looked like love—in Alison's eyes that evening had made every moment worth it.

Alison took two Tylenol before pulling her comforter to her chin. Her shoulders ached. Sleep overtook her before she could even finish the prayer she started.

Tuesday morning, Alison woke up to the sound of footsteps above her room. With a groan she maneuvered her drained body into a hot shower. When she entered the kitchen, Jeremy stood at the stove, a frittata in the skillet.

She smiled and sat down at the kitchen table. "I think I'm the one who's supposed to cook you breakfast, Jeremy," she teased. "It's not called a bed and breakfast for nothing, you know."

He smiled, slid a frittata on a plate and placed it in front of her. "I'm not exactly a guest this week, Ali. At least, I hope I'm not."

She caught his hand before he walked back to the stove. "Do you feel at home here, Jeremy?" She was truly curious. But at that moment, Nicholas slouched into the kitchen, moaning about how he was definitely too tired to go to school. Alison had to direct her attention to the sluggish eight-year-old boy who needed to down breakfast quickly and do something about his bedhead hair before she drove him to school, tired or not.

Because most of the outside repairs had been tackled the day before, Jeremy spent that morning reorganizing Alison's kitchen to make it more functional. When his friend Crey, another chef from Romano's, arrived with three bags of ingredients and groceries, Jeremy went outside to finish a few projects while Crey taught Alison some simple but elegant and flavorful new breakfast recipes to add to her menu. He went over everything with her from staple ingredients she always needed to have on hand to which fruits and jams complemented which dishes best. They talked about the expense of ingredients and how to create a dining experience that worked effectively and smoothly. He gave her tips on plating and presentation and the correct way to position a table setting.

When she checked her email before lunch, Alison was thrilled to see that three reservation requests had come in, two for the weekend approaching and one for the middle of the following week. The ads must be driving interest. As they worked together to finish painting the bathroom on the main floor, she told Jeremy the good news.

"Well, we need to have everything in shipshape order by Friday then," he said. Alison nodded, holding back a smile over Jeremy's oh-so-serious manner.

Wednesday, Alison spent three hours on the phone with Jeremy's friend Eddie as he walked her through suggestions to make the B&B website more user-friendly. Alison felt like she needed an entire college course on online marketing to have any clue of what she was doing, but she took notes and tried to follow Eddie's instructions to the letter. She appreciated his ideas of joining with a third-party online marketing site for more exposure and buying ads on popular travel sites.

She spent the rest of the day sprucing up the guest bedrooms; Jennifer had left Alison strict instructions on how to incorporate a festive look to the rooms for the holidays without overwhelming guests. Alison hung simple white wreaths in every window of the house. When she stood outside later and looked at the exterior view of the B&B, she couldn't believe how such easy changes had made the house seem so inviting. She walked out to the road, to take in the full sight of the house, and noticed that the B&B sign by the street looked worn and dated.

I never even notice the sign anymore. It looks terrible.

The paint was faded and chipped. The words *Mountain View* were barely legible from a distance.

"Ali!" Jeremy yelled from the garage. "I need another extension cord!"

"Coming!"

I'll have to figure out what to do with the sign later.

It had been Jeremy's idea to string white Christmas lights all through the large fir tree right by the house. Alison helped him find another extension cord and then strung the lights with him.

"It's getting colder out here," she said above the sound of the wind.

"Cold front comes in tomorrow," Jeremy reminded her. "We should have snow by Friday night. It'll be a gorgeous weekend in the mountains for your guests."

Alison nodded, tremors of excitement running through her at the thought of entertaining guests now that the house looked so beautiful. She stood back as Jeremy plugged in the lights. She knew he was just testing to make sure everything worked right, but as the tree lit up, she clapped with unrestrained joy.

Christmas had come back to her house.

Chapter 23

"**I** wish I didn't have to leave," Jeremy said Friday morning, frustrated with himself.

"Jeremy, you have a job to do. I completely understand. You've worked so hard all week! The restaurant needs you. Leo needs you."

Jeremy shook his head. He'd planned to stay through the following weekend and help Alison cook for the new guests, but when he'd called Leo, he discovered that Margo had taken off for a family emergency and one of the cooks at the Franklin Street restaurant was ill. So Leo was cooking at the other location and he needed Jeremy at the Fifteenth Street restaurant.

"Will we see you before Christmas?" she asked, hope in her voice. Jeremy pulled Ali into a hug.

"I'll try my best to be back. You have guests next week, right?"

"Yes. Both sets arrive tonight and will be here until Sunday afternoon. Then we have a family coming in Wednesday and staying until Friday. And the following weekend, too! We got another email reservation last night. And then we have that couple showing up the day after Christmas." Alison's smile was contagious. "I feel like…I don't know how to explain it. I want to sing 'Joy to the World' as loud as I can."

Jeremy smiled down at her and noticed her eyes mist over. "I can't thank you enough. You made all this happen,

Jeremy. I don't know whether business will keep picking up or not, but I feel so encouraged."

"I'm glad, Ali. I'm going to miss you and Nicholas."

"We're going to miss you, too."

I love you, Ali.

The words were just below the surface, but Jeremy couldn't bring himself to say them. *It's too soon. She'll freak out.*

A light snow fell as he drove back through the mountains. When he reached Denver, the snow started coming down hard. Jeremy made it home just in time to change clothes and get to the restaurant for dinner prep. After a long night of steady orders, he went home, fairly certain he'd passed the point of extreme exhaustion hours earlier. He woke up the next morning to a completely snow-covered Denver. Jeremy scrambled eggs and sat down to breakfast alone, looking out the window at the few flurries that kept falling.

I wish I was in Estes Park building up a fire at the B&B and having breakfast with Alison and Nicholas, then cooking up some of my favorite winter recipes and enjoying the lights on that enormous Christmas tree.

He chuckled at the thought of Ali's choice for a Christmas tree. She hadn't been lying when she'd said she wasn't a Charlie Brown Christmas tree kind of girl. Jeremy looked around his sparse apartment, realizing that he hadn't put up even a hint of garland. There were no signs of Christmas having arrived at his apartment.

He didn't really care. In truth, he hoped he'd be spending Christmas morning at the B&B. Alison hadn't asked him and he wasn't quite sure how to invite himself to such an important holiday gathering.

I'll just wait. If she doesn't say anything, then she's probably reserving Christmas for her and Nicholas and her parents. He could always drive down to Santa Fe on

Christmas Eve. Romano's would be closed on Christmas Eve and Christmas Day.

Jeremy sipped his coffee and checked the clock. He had a handful of Christmas presents to buy before work that evening. He'd wanted to buy Nicholas a fly rod from the very first day they'd fished together. The kid liked fishing almost as much as Jeremy did. Jeremy couldn't wait to see the look on Nic's face when he opened it. Jeremy put his coffee mug in the sink and went to get ready to face the craziness of shopping in Denver at Christmastime.

Tuesday morning Alison spread more flour on the kitchen counter. Their guests had left Sunday afternoon and Estes Park had received so much snow Monday night that schools were cancelled.

"Not so many sprinkles, Nicholas!"

Nicholas didn't look up from his workstation at the other end of the counter. They were making Christmas cookies for Wednesday's soup kitchen.

"*Mom*," Nicholas said. "I know what people like, and people like sprinkles. Trust me on this."

She bit back a laugh. "Well, try to keep it to a minimum or we'll run out. We need to make enough to set out for our guests tomorrow, too."

"It's been pretty cool, hasn't it, having so many people at our house lately? Everybody from church and Jeremy and his friends and those people this weekend and now more people tomorrow," Nicholas said, pausing to take a bite of the cookie he'd just covered in sprinkles. Alison rolled out more dough and grabbed an angel-shaped cookie cutter.

"I think it's been wonderful."

"Is Jeremy spending Christmas with us?"

"Oh, Nic. I'm sure he's planning on spending Christmas with his mom and his sister."

"What if he wants to spend it with us?"

Alison looked down at the cookie form she'd just cut out. "Do you want me to invite him?" she asked.

Nicholas nodded. "Sure. Don't you want to?"

More than anything.

The timer on the stove beeped and Alison pulled out a pan of warm gingerbread cookies. She set them aside to cool. "You know, I think that would be really nice. Thanks for thinking of that, Nicholas."

"I have good ideas," he said with a shrug. "Like the sprinkles."

The next morning Alison dropped off five dozen sugar and gingerbread cookies at the church.

"I'd stay to help, but we have guests checking in at noon," she said in a rush to Lenora.

"Go on, Alison. We're fine. Thanks for bringing the cookies!"

Alison trudged through the snow back to her SUV and headed home to clean up before her guests arrived. Once she'd welcomed the young couple with two elementary-aged children, Alison got Nicholas—school had been cancelled again—settled watching a movie in the basement and she opened her laptop to check her email.

A message from Jeremy was waiting for her.

Ali,

Any chance you could make a reservation for a couple of friends of mine? I'll send you all the info later, though I want to pick up the tab for them so the reservation needs to be under my credit card. They were hoping to come up Monday the twenty-second. One night only. Two adults. I know it's close to Christmas so it's okay if you'd rather not take visitors.

Missing you every day,

Jeremy

P.S. I got Nic a fly rod for Christmas. What size fishing vest would he wear?

A fly rod for Nicholas! Alison's heart warmed. *Thank you, Lord.*

Alison quickly typed back that she'd be happy to have his guests come up for a night, then added Nic's vest size. After a moment, she typed one more line.

By the way, we'd love for you to join us for Christmas. But I warn you, you'll have to help in the kitchen, Chef.

Alison sent the email and then joined Nicholas in the living room.

"Mom, *How the Grinch Stole Christmas!* is about to come on. Want to watch it?"

Alison grinned and walked to the kitchenette. "It's a date. I'll make the popcorn." Alison popped some microwave popcorn, poured it in a bowl and curled up on the sofa next to Nicholas.

"Hey, what should we get Jeremy for Christmas?" Nicholas asked before stuffing a handful of popcorn in his mouth.

"Hmm. Good question. Any ideas Mr. 'I have good ideas'?" Alison tickled him, and Nicholas howled with laughter.

"It needs to be something really great," Nicholas said once he calmed down, taking another handful of popcorn. Alison popped a piece in her mouth and nodded.

"I agree. Let's think about it. But we don't have much time. Christmas is less than two weeks away."

Long after Nicholas had gone to sleep, Alison racked her brain, trying to think of what to give Jeremy for Christmas. She wanted to give him a special gift, but nothing came to mind. She thought of all that Jeremy had done for her and the B&B.

What in the world can I get him?

Chapter 24

"Who's coming, Jeremy? I couldn't have heard you right." Alison froze. She gripped the cell phone to her ear.

"It's going to be fine, Ali. Trust me. You wanted exposure for the B&B. This is going to make that happen."

"You're saying Mandy Seymour of *Denver Lifestyle* magazine and the *Take Me There* network is coming to my house tomorrow? She's the friend you booked the reservation for? And you didn't think that was an important detail to share with me immediately?" Her voice grew more shrill with each question.

"Mandy Romano. She only goes by Seymour as her pen name. And not just her. She, Leo and the baby are coming on Monday. Little Antonio is staying the night with Ethan and Isabella, but they're bringing Olivia with them. This is a great opportunity for you. I can't believe they actually agreed to make the trip this close to Christmas!"

"Me either," Alison replied numbly.

"I have a feeling a review from Mandy will boost interest considerably come the new year."

"That's assuming she writes me a *good* review, Jeremy," Alison reminded him.

"I have faith in you, Alison." Her heart melted just a tad, knowing that Jeremy did indeed have faith in her.

"Okay," she said, the news sinking in. "What do I make for her?"

"Whatever you want! Make that breakfast casserole I like so much."

"When are you coming back?" Alison asked, trying to keep any signs of desperation out of her voice.

"I'm definitely coming for Christmas. I won't be able to be there by tomorrow, but I'm aiming for Tuesday afternoon. I have a lot of vacation time stored up, which is a good thing because I seem to be using it right and left. I want to be sure to be there for Christmas Eve with you and Nicholas."

"Oh good! You can go to the candlelight Christmas Eve service with us!"

"That sounds perfect. Maybe we can do some last-minute shopping together when I get there. I'll need to pick up a few things for Christmas dinner. You have a turkey, right?"

"I do," Alison assured him. An idea took root in her thoughts. A gift of sorts. Alison hung up the phone, ready to re-clean everything and plan her menu for Mrs. Mandy Romano.

By the time Monday arrived, Alison was a bundle of nerves. She paced the floor. The house smelled of gingerbread and sugar cookies; soft Christmas carols played on the stereo; more snow had fallen, leaving the outside view of the house as scenic as Alison could have hoped it would be. The large fir tree outside was lit, and Alison had built up a crackling fire in the living room fireplace. In the Dove guestroom peppermint candles glowed. Alison had pulled back the drapes so Mandy and Leo could take in the full view of the snow-covered woods and the cold, rushing river behind the house.

She steeled herself when she heard the knock at the door. *Be professional. Don't be nervous. You can do this.*

She opened the door wide and smiled. "Welcome to the Mountain View Bed and Breakfast!"

A handsome man with thick dark hair stood on her doorstep holding a baby carrier.

"Come in quickly out of the cold!" Alison said, holding the door open wide.

"Thank you. I'm Leo Romano. This sleeping little one is Olivia." He set the baby carrier down gently.

"I'm Mandy Romano." A woman with long brown hair and a warm smile walked in behind Leo. She dusted snow from her knee-length camel-colored coat.

"I'll get our bags, Mandy. Olivia's out like a light." Leo disappeared back outside.

"I hope you'll make yourself at home, Mandy," Alison said, trying not to act as stiff as she felt. "Let me show you around."

Mandy followed her slowly through the living room and into the kitchen, then upstairs, while Alison explained that they had access to everything on the first floor and that she and Nicholas lived in the basement. Alison showed her each bedroom, finishing with the Dove room. Mandy walked straight to the window. The last light of day spilled out over the mountains.

"You have a river!"

Alison joined her by the window. "Yes. The river is the main reason Connor and I bought the house. There's something soothing about a river."

"I couldn't agree more. I grew up in Evergreen, Colorado, and we lived right by a river. Some days, I still feel desperate to be near one. I'll drive to Evergreen and just sit out on the deck at my parents' house, listening to the water."

"When Jeremy first came out here, I could tell that his soul was thirsting for a river."

"I know the feeling," Mandy replied. She turned away from the window and walked around the room, then peeked her head into the bathroom before setting her purse on the writing desk and running her fingers over the sitting chair.

"Alison, this is lovely."

Alison breathed a sigh of relief. "Thank you."

Mandy faced her with a knowing smile. "You don't have to worry, you know. Jeremy's been singing your praises for weeks. And his words hold a lot of weight with me and Leo."

Alison flushed. "Well, I appreciate you coming more than you know."

"Any friend of Jeremy's is a friend of mine." Mandy reached out and squeezed Alison's hand. "I'm looking forward to breakfast in the morning!"

Leo pushed the door open with the baby carrier in one hand and a duffel bag in the other. "I need to set up the portable baby crib," he whispered. Alison left them to get settled and made her way downstairs.

She went to the basement, where Nicholas was playing video games. After a while, she heard footsteps on the main floor and soft voices, but she didn't go back upstairs. She wanted to give Mandy and Leo free rein of the house.

Alison woke extra early the next morning to prepare the breakfast casserole Jeremy was so fond of and to set out fruit, toast, jam and pastries on the buffet table in the dining room. She brewed fresh coffee and set out tea bags and hot water, just in case they weren't coffee drinkers. She added pitchers of water and orange juice. She stood back and admired her work, thinking that Crey's tips had definitely helped with her presentation.

At eight on the dot, Mandy and Leo came down for breakfast. "Olivia's asleep, thankfully. She was up a few times last night, so she should be worn out," Mandy told Alison.

"I would imagine you both are, too, then," Alison said sympathetically.

"This should help," Leo said with a smile as he pointed to the coffee. Nicholas came upstairs for a minute and Alison introduced him to both Leo and Mandy. She directed him to a plate of breakfast she'd held back for him in the kitchen, then quickly shooed him downstairs. She refilled the coffee pot while the couple grabbed plates and looked over the contents on the buffet table. At around nine, everyone heard the cry of a baby, and Mandy and Leo went back upstairs to tend to Olivia. Alison cleaned up the remnants of the meal.

Soon the three of them came to the first floor, all bundled up and ready to leave to Alison's surprise.

"Oh, we're just running into town, Alison," Mandy assured her. "I want to know what the surrounding attractions are for guests. It's been awhile since I've been to Estes Park. Any places you recommend for lunch?" Alison gave a few options and supplied them with plenty of brochures.

As they left, Alison stood in the doorway and wondered what Mandy had thought of her breakfast. She turned and finished cleaning the kitchen, checking the clock constantly and wishing Jeremy would arrive soon. Nicholas was bored by this point, so Alison drove him over to Michelle and Shawn's house, promising to pick him up that night after dinner. She rushed back home to keep an eye on things. The Romanos returned a little after noon, having already stopped for lunch. Alison set out cookies and hot cocoa for a snack and again went downstairs.

From the basement, she finally heard a knock at the front door. She raced up the stairs and threw open the door.

Her favorite chef stood on the porch.

"How's it going?" he asked. Alison pulled him inside.

"I'm not sure. I've barely seen them today. They had breakfast, then went to explore the town."

"Good! Estes Park is a fun place. Can I get a hug, by the way?"

Alison stopped for a moment and smiled back at Jeremy. She put her arms around his neck and gave him a squeeze. He managed to steal a kiss before letting her go.

"The lights on the tree out front were a stroke of genius. It looks great," he whispered.

"*Your* stroke of genius," Alison chuckled.

"Jeremy!" Leo said as he walked down the hallway. The two friends shook hands. Alison enjoyed seeing the camaraderie between Jeremy and Leo. The two were obviously fast friends by the way they ribbed each other and seemed so comfortable together. Mandy waved for the group to join her in the kitchen; Olivia was in her arms.

"You guys come in here!" she called out. "Alison's made the best sugar cookies I've ever tasted. I want the recipe for this frosting."

The three of them joined her in the kitchen.

Leo reached for a snowman cookie and devoured the whole thing in two bites.

"You could sell these by the millions, Alison," he said, grabbing another. "I'm serious. If you'll send me a box to take home with me, I bet Ethan and Isabella would order dozens for the café."

"Like they'd survive the trip home!" Mandy exclaimed. "You know we'd finish the box off before we left Estes Park city limits, Leo!"

Alison smiled. "Thanks, guys. I will say they take a lot of effort to make, but the result is always worth it. The recipe comes from my mother-in-law, Diana, actually. Every Christmas she used to host a cookie party. All the women of the family would spend an entire day baking—we'd have workstations for rolling out the dough, then frosting and decorating. Those are wonderful memories for me. This year Nicholas was my helper, so the decorating is a little interesting."

Everyone chuckled at the stack of sprinkle-inundated cookies. The snowman cookie that Alison reached for had one eye and looked as though he'd been dipped in blue sprinkles. Alison watched as Mandy passed Olivia over to Jeremy, who seemed perfectly at ease holding the baby.

Alison worked hard to take her gaze away from the picture of Jeremy holding tiny Olivia, talking to her softly and rubbing her back.

If I wasn't in love with Jeremy Mitchell before this moment, I'm definitely a goner now.

Chapter 25

"I'm telling you, Ali, you have nothing to worry about. Mandy had a great time! And she told me she wants the recipe to your breakfast casserole." Jeremy tried to reassure Alison. The two of them were sitting together on the sofa. Mandy and Leo and the baby had left an hour before.

"What are we making for dinner?" Jeremy asked. "And what time are we picking up Nicholas? I can't wait to see him."

Alison looked as though she wasn't quite ready to stop processing Mandy's visit, but she switched gears.

"I have plans for us for dinner. And we're picking up Nicholas afterward. So you should change into something *much* warmer. I will, too. I'll meet you at the door in fifteen minutes."

"Warmer?" Jeremy looked down at his jeans. "Where are we going?"

Alison jumped up and winked at him. "Just follow directions, Chef."

With a grin, Jeremy rushed upstairs, deciding to add long johns under his jeans, an extra undershirt and thicker socks. He switched his long-sleeved cotton shirt for a thick sweater and then pulled on his heavy coat and headed downstairs.

Alison stood at the door, bundled in a warm coat and thick boots. She held gloves and hats for both of them.

"Where are we headed?" he asked again once they were

in her SUV and headed toward Estes Park; the suspense was killing him.

Alison just shook her head. "You'll see." She turned a corner and they entered Main Street. "This is sort of your Christmas present. I had a really hard time coming up with an idea of what to get you."

Jeremy's interest spiked. He enjoyed surprises. What he appreciated most was the thought that went into the planning. The fact that Alison had planned out a surprise for him—Jeremy's heart fell just a little harder for her. She pulled into one of the parking lots on Main Street.

"We have to pick up supplies first," she informed him. "It's cold out, so put your gloves and hat on."

Hand in gloved hand, they walked down the sidewalk and Jeremy whistled through the night air.

"Now this is what I call a small-town Christmas. I love it," he said, and Alison's smile told him she understood perfectly. Against the backdrop of snow-immersed mountains beneath a navy sky, a canopy of Christmas lights reached from one side of the street to the other. Christmas wreaths hung from every light post, and standing on a street corner, a group of carolers sang "God Rest Ye Merry Gentlemen" a cappella. The lights of shops and restaurants illuminated the darkness and made the town feel vibrant and alive. People bustled here and there, shopping bags on their arms and coffee cups warming their hands.

The mountain town was immersed in the season of Christmas, and Jeremy ached to be part of it. He'd missed this in the city—the community feeling, the holiday excitement in the air at a slower pace. The lights, the smells, the sounds, the decorations—walking down Main Street with Alison, Jeremy felt as though he were part of the season here.

"Here we are." Alison led him into a small café. "Jason?" she called out. A Hispanic man with a very full goatee came out from the back, an apron tied around his waist and a backward baseball cap on his head.

"Right on time," he said with a smile. He reached from behind the counter and handed her a picnic basket.

"Thanks so much. I'll get the basket back to you next week," Alison told him.

"Don't worry about it, Ali. Merry Christmas!" he said, and Alison and Jeremy did the same. Alison promptly handed Jeremy the picnic basket to carry.

"Back to the car," she instructed.

"I feel like we're on a scavenger hunt," Jeremy told her. She kept her lips pursed and Jeremy knew she was enjoying the adventure as much as he was.

She drove a little ways out of town; Jeremy wondered where they could be going but kept himself from asking again. Finally she turned into the driveway of an old, large farmhouse.

A man who looked to be in his early fifties stood on the porch, leaning against a post. "Hey, Gary!" Alison called out. She turned back to Jeremy. "Oh! Bring the picnic basket, will you?"

Jeremy grabbed the basket and followed her to where Gary was standing.

"You two ready? I hope you dressed warm enough," he said.

Alison nodded.

"Follow me," he told them. They walked to the side of the house and Jeremy stopped mid-step.

"Is he Santa?" Jeremy whispered and Alison giggled. They stood in front of a gorgeous white sleigh hooked up to a large bay mare.

"Climb in, lovebirds," Gary said with a chuckle as he took his seat in front and gathered up the reins. Alison climbed in first, then took the basket from Jeremy. The seat was covered in fur, and two large quilts were waiting for them. Jeremy sat next to Alison, and they bundled under the blankets.

"Giddyap, Belle." Gary clucked his tongue and the horse started to trot, pulling the sleigh through the deep snow.

"Gary owns a tree farm. He's one of my dad's closest friends so he was nice enough to take us on a night ride," Alison explained, setting the basket on her lap and opening it. She pulled out a thermos and handed it to Jeremy.

"The best tomato basil soup you'll ever taste," she said. On a cloth napkin, she set out two roast beef sandwiches, then pulled out a thermos of her own soup. The bells on the sleigh jingled as Gary led them through rows of tall Christmas trees. The moon, so full and bright, lit up the night sky. Jeremy sipped his soup and ate the sandwich, talking softly with Alison and drinking in the perfection of winter in the mountains. The sleigh slowed to a stop right past the line of trees.

"Here's your spot, Ali-girl," Gary said.

"Your spot?" Jeremy echoed. Alison smiled.

"I've been coming here since I was a teenager. We'd come get a tree from Gary and Linda every Christmas. And he'd bring me and my parents way out here because I like the view."

An expanse of snow stretched out in the distance, meeting the base of the mountains. Jeremy leaned back and gasped at the sight above him. Alison snuggled next to him and they just gazed upward. From Jeremy's line of view, the sky had never looked so endless. The mind-blowing number of stars looked like a huge blanket God had thrown out over the world.

Other than the woman sitting next to him, Jeremy had never seen anything so beautiful.

"Thank you for sharing this place with me, Ali."

Alison rested her head on his shoulder.

"Merry Christmas, Jeremy."

It's time.

"Alison, I think you know I've fallen in love with you."

She sat back up. Gary jumped from his seat.

"I'll give you two a moment," he said, walking up closer to the horse and pulling an apple out of his pocket. Jeremy turned to look at Ali. She looked at odds with herself.

"I never thought I'd love anyone again—not after losing Connor."

"I understand," he said, his heart sinking.

"But I was wrong."

Jeremy froze…and not from the cold.

"Jeremy, I love you, too. You asked if I'd ever be willing to leave Estes Park. I brought you here to show you why I love this place so much. The mountains are part of me. But not the only part. You've given me hope that I can make the B&B a success. And I want to try. But if it doesn't work out—and maybe even if it does—I want you to know I'm open to moving. I can't make any promises about that. But I'm open."

Jeremy listened silently, knowing how much it took for Alison to say the words. He put an arm around her and they both looked back up at the vast, glittering stars above them, God's twinkle lights.

"Could you share your dream of running the B&B, Ali?"

She was quiet and Jeremy waited, feeling like his whole future hinged on her answer.

"I could share it with you," she finally answered, her words certain. "But I have Nicholas to think about. I need him to be comfortable with that idea before we can move forward."

Jeremy nodded. "We'll make this a gradual transition. How does that sound? For now, I'll stay in Denver. But over the next few months, I want to move out here to be with you guys. It means everything to me that you're open to the thought of moving to Denver, Ali." Jeremy looked back at the sky. "But I feel like I belong here, too. I know what you mean about connecting to this place. I'll get an apartment. I'll find a job and we'll go from there. I want you to be completely sure before we go any further. But you have to know that I want to marry you. I'm moving here because I want you and me and Nicholas to be a family."

He could hear Alison sniffling next to him. Worried, Jeremy turned so they faced each other. But through her tears, a smile reached all the way to Alison's eyes. With relief, he pulled her to him and kissed her, a cold kiss that warmed them both.

Alison sighed. "I never thought God would give this to me again—this kind of love. But He did. I want us to be a family too, Jeremy. If and when the time is right."

Jeremy wiped a tear from Alison's face. "A family for Christmas. It's the best present I've ever received."

Gary climbed back in the sleigh and flicked the reins.

"About time, you two. I was near frozen up there with Belle. Let's get back to the house. Linda has hot chocolate and homemade pecan pie waiting for us."

Chapter 26

One year later. Christmas Eve.

"I think the bow tie looks funny."

Jeremy turned and grinned at Nicholas, who was fidgeting with the tie around his neck.

"You look great, buddy. Do you have the ring?"

Nicholas pulled a box out of his pocket. "Got it. Are you nervous?"

Jeremy straightened his own tie before sitting on the chair in the Dove room. "Not really. I've been waiting for this day for a while. Sit down, Nic. There's something I want to say to you."

Nicholas sat on the bed.

"You know how happy I am to be marrying your mom today," Jeremy said seriously. "I love her very much. And I love you, too."

Nicholas nodded.

"But I'm not trying to replace your dad. I know he was a wonderful man."

Nicholas looked at Jeremy, his face a little shy and thoughtful. "I was thinking…maybe you could be my dad, too. If you want."

Jeremy tried to swallow, but the lump in his throat made it difficult. He took a breath to steady himself and looked back at Nicholas.

"I would be honored to be your dad, Nicholas. And to have you as my son."

Nicholas jumped up and put his arms around Jeremy. Jeremy closed his eyes and held the boy in his arms.

I've just become a father. Lord, thank you. Help me to be the dad Nicholas needs.

"Jeremy, it's time," Leo poked his head in the room.

"Got it," Jeremy said as he looked at Leo. "Nicholas and I are on our way. Right, Nic?"

Nicholas stood tall in his tuxedo. "Right, Dad."

Jeremy paused, not wanting to ever forget how he felt right then. He looked at Leo and knew he understood the weight of the moment. Jeremy already felt like crying and he hadn't even seen Ali yet. Leo looked as though he were holding back tears, too.

The door pushed open further and Ethan walked in. "Now's not the time to keep your lady waiting, Jeremy."

Jeremy nodded. He and Nicholas filed out of the room and went downstairs. It was to be the first wedding held at the newly renamed Sweet River Bed and Breakfast. A brand-new sign—a wedding gift from Eli and Jolene—stood proudly out by the road. The name change had been Alison's idea—a way to begin anew, a fresh start with a new dream that belonged to Jeremy and Alison.

Jeremy and Nicholas positioned themselves in front of the fireplace next to Pastor Daniel. Guests spilled into every available space on the first floor. Alison had wanted a Christmas Eve wedding, and they'd figured only a handful of family members could attend. But once again, they'd been reminded that family shows up for one another. Jennifer had transformed the house into a wonderland, fit for a beautiful holiday wedding. Leo and Mandy and Ethan and Isabella and a host of others from Denver had insisted on attending, as well as Jeremy's immediate family, and it seemed as though every member of River Community Church was packed into the B&B.

The house went silent in one hush as the "Carol of the Bells" began to play. Jeremy looked at his mother and June and Dylan sitting on the front row. His mother's eyes shone with pride.

Jeremy couldn't breathe as Alison rounded the corner, her hand holding her father's arm. Her simple white wedding gown touched the floor and her blond hair was swept to the side in an elegant twist with tiny white flowers woven through it. In her free hand, she held a bouquet of red roses.

They stopped in front of him. Alison leaned down and kissed Nicholas's cheek, whispering in his ear before stepping forward and allowing Jeremy to take her hand in his.

"What are you thinking?" she whispered as they turned to face Pastor Daniel. Jeremy leaned close so only she could hear him.

"That I'm going to wake up on Christmas morning and have Alison Taylor-Mitchell next to me."

Alison smiled and tightened her grip on his hand. "Sounds like a holiday to remember, my love."

* * * * *

REQUEST YOUR FREE BOOKS!

2 FREE INSPIRATIONAL NOVELS
PLUS 2
FREE
MYSTERY GIFTS

Love Inspired

LIDIR13R